ALSO BY NIKITA SINGH

The Promise
Someone Like You
The Unreasonable Fellows

PENGUIN BOOKS

ACCIDENTALLY IN LOVE

Nikita Singh is the bestselling author of six novels, including *Love @ Facebook*, *Accidentally in Love* and *The Promise*. She has co-authored two books with Durjoy Datta, titled *If It's Not Forever . . .* and *Someone Like You*. She has also contributed to the books in the *Backbenchers* series. She was born in Patna and grew up in Indore, from where she graduated in pharmacy. She is currently based in New Delhi, where she works as an editor at a leading publishing house.

Nikita received a Live India Young Achievers Award in 2013. With a library stocked with over 12,000 books, she is a voracious reader and adores her collection of fantasy novels. She is a cricket enthusiast and enjoys a good cardio workout.

NIKITA SINGH

Accidentally in Love

Penguin
metro reads

An imprint of Penguin Random House

PENGUIN METRO READS

USA | Canada | UK | Ireland | Australia
New Zealand | India | South Africa | China | Singapore

Penguin Metro Reads is part of the Penguin Random House group of companies
whose addresses can be found at global.penguinrandomhouse.com

Published by Penguin Random House India Pvt. Ltd
4th Floor, Capital Tower 1, MG Road,
Gurugram 122 002, Haryana, India

Penguin
Random House
India

First published by Grapevine India Publishers 2011
Published in Penguin Metro Reads by Penguin Books India 2014

Copyright © Nikita Singh 2014

ISBN 9780143421641

Typeset in Bembo Std by Eleven Arts, Delhi
Printed at Manipal Technologies Limited, India

www.penguin.co.in

MIX
Paper | Supporting
responsible forestry
FSC® C043100

This is a legitimate digitally printed version of the book and therefore might not
have certain extra finishing on the cover.

Dedicated to Maa!

And Bullet—the imaginary golden
retriever she never let me pet for real!

Contents

x   Contents

Acknowledgments

When you write a book, yes, it is you who is doing the actual writing, but if certain people aren't there with you to do certain things, the whole writing process becomes such a pain! I would like to thank these people for being there, when this book was written.

My family—for freeing me from my daily chores and letting me work in peace. Well. Most of the times, at least. Papa, for listening to me patiently when I don't stop talking gibberish! Maa, for serving my meals next to my laptop, on my desk, three times a day. And taking the plates back. Nishant Malay, for being rude to me. Always. Why do elder brothers have to be so mean?

Since essentially I am an extremely lazy person, I always need someone to sit on my head to make me work. I would like to thank the Grapevine India family for doing that for me, and so much more. Thank you Durjoy Datta—for your cute dimple and for putting in the cheeky one-liners in this book. And Sachin Garg—for your valuable inputs, and for believing in me, way more than I do.

For always being by my side and making my world a better (and funnier) place, I want to thank all my cousins—Kumar Abhinav, Prishita Singh, Tushar Deep, Vishal Kumar, Abhimanyu Singh, Shaina Singh, Shreela Singh and Pooja Singh.

For the 'honest and very useful' reviews—Alka Singh, Rohan Rai, Abhay Mishra and Pratham Jain. Seriously people, if you hadn't lied and said that it rocks, the book would've been way better! You hamper my growth as a writer!

Others, who sent random messages once or twice in their lifetime, asking, 'So? How is your book coming along?' I would like to thank—Ashay Shukla, Viyali Michael, Nidhi Sharma, Deepika Rathore, Sameer Joshi, Amresh Kumar and Santosh Kumar. Love you all.

A note of thanks to people who read and like my books and blog posts, and follow me on Facebook, Twitter and other social networks. You guys make every pain I face while writing worth it.

Most importantly—Guruji, Sri Sri Paramhansa Yogananda, for his teachings and blessings, which give me courage at the worst times and keep me going.

PROLOGUE
Love . . . and Other Basic Calculations!

Love is just a calculation. Before you decide to get into 'something special' with someone, there are certain parameters you calculate and then arrive at a conclusion, depending on which you may or may not have a relationship.

First, you calculate if the other person is good enough for you to date or not. Is he tall enough? Is she hot enough? Is he rich enough? Is she hot enough? Is he interesting/funny enough? Is she hot enough? Is he intelligent enough? Is she hot enough?

Most people you meet never match the criteria you set. They are a total reject. But then, there are a few, who *do* fulfil your criteria. And then, another set of calculations start. You calculate if getting into something 'special' with that person would affect your mental peace.

Would he treat me well? Would she be good at making out? Would he care enough? Would she be too demanding? Would he be too possessive? Would she be too sluttish? Would he give me enough time? Would she be too clingy?

And then—the most popular question of all time—*would this interfere with my career?*

And what if your special one lives miles apart from you? You would still do anything and everything to make it work. The beginning is awesome, with you never leaving your IM, telling your love how much you miss his/her presence. But soon your love begins to grow old, and you start to struggle. And then again—career.

But you *like* each other! So what is the solution? A strictly physical, open relationship, that does not demand too much of your time and does not have the hassle of a real relationship. And you get all the perks! What can be better?

Ha! As if love follows a plan!

I am not saying that this book has a story that has something to do with what I have been saying. And definitely not in the same sequence. But my point stays—love can*not* be planned.

It is like gravity. You can try to go against it, but you really can't. You can jump off a cliff, trying to fly, but you will *not*. You will fall. It is inevitable. Similarly, falling in love cannot be prevented. It is inevitable too. And if you are smart enough to recognize that it is real, you should be smart enough to fight for it and never let it go. Life does not give you too many second chances.

Don't let love ever pass you by.

This is a story of people finding true love, losing it and . . . well, read the book to know the rest!

The Glamour

1 July 2011

'Chhavi!' I heard someone call my name.

'Mmm?' I murmured sleepily.

'Wake up!' Vatsala shouted in my ear. 'We have to go to the studio.'

'Why?' I asked.

'Because we have to work.'

'Work? But I don't have anything today.'

'You don't, but *I* do. My first shoot. And you promised you would come with me,' Vatsala said.

'Hmm,' I tried to block out her voice and get back to sleep.

'I have prepared breakfast. Do you want me to serve it to you here?'

'*What?*' I said and woke up with a jerk. *Vatsala prepared breakfast?* We had been sharing an apartment since the past couple of weeks and never once had she so much as stirred a ladle. All she does is peek into the vessels occasionally, while I am cooking, and crib about my slow speed. To think that she

1

prepared breakfast for the two of us . . . that she actually even woke up so early . . . 'Wow. You really cooked?'

'Actually . . . no! I was just trying to wake you up,' she laughed. 'But please do cook something quickly. I am starving.'

'As usual,' I said and made my way to the kitchen. It was amazing that she could eat so much and still maintain that figure. I, for one, had to work out every single day to make sure agencies kept hiring me. Being a model has its own disadvantages, you see? I had been modelling since two years and had never gained a single stone. I was actually quite proud of the fact, but still wished that I didn't have to work for it. Having an impeccable figure with absolutely zero effort? That's the dream!

'So, what should I wear?' Vatsala asked.

'They will arrange an outfit. You don't have to worry.' It was Vatsala's first day of work at the studio. I work at Metro News, covering the tiny sports slot of the prime time news. That is the only permanent position I hold anywhere. Metro News had recently hired Vatsala to anchor their weekend show about the entertainment industry. In fact, it was at her interview with our team when I first met her. I had been looking for a flatmate and she had been looking for a place to live. That's how we ended up sharing an apartment.

'Yeah, but what do I wear *to* the studio?'

'PJs, shorts, whatever! Doesn't matter,' I replied.

'Really?' She seemed amazed.

'Yes. Really. No one is going to care what you wear to the studio. Why would they? They just care about your on-screen appearance. Just wear any pair of jeans and get ready.'

'Okay,' she said, and turned to leave.

She seemed really nervous about this. Although, she didn't need to be. I was there when she was being auditioned. She was awesome. Everyone at the set was a big fan of hers already. In fact, they didn't even audition the remaining participants after her. Yes, she was *that* good.

But of course, the first-timer nervousness cannot be shaken off. I remember my first time. The first offer I had received was when I was still in Kolkata. To my shock, my family was not against the idea of my modelling. But slowly, I understood the real reason.

I had been a troublesome kid all my life. They just figured that I would not listen to anything that they would have to say, anyway. They had lost all arguments before, so they didn't want to get into another one. So even though they were not happy about it, they did their best to mask it.

So I had flown to Mumbai. And the first time I heard the director say 'action' into his microphone, I had totally forgotten what I was supposed to do. I had frozen and had wanted to run back home!

But that had not happened again since. And after that, my career had gone on a roll. I had been flooded by modelling offers for advertisements for products of all sorts and from all kinds of sectors. I was that type of model; the one who is cast in advertisements—still and motion. The reason I never tried my luck in ramp modelling was because I knew that at 5'5" high I didn't have much of a bright future there. Plus, ramp models have to be *really* thin. I liked my version of thin—the I-still-have-boobs version!

Anyway, it always thrilled me to see my pictures on hoardings and in magazines. And it always felt amazing when people recognized me from the ads they saw on TV. It was very fulfilling. And I had been pretty content with what I had going. Until recently.

Since the last few months, the number of offers I received had started to dip. A major number of the offers I received were for print modelling. I started disappearing from the face of television, and it had started to worry me. I already knew that the career of a model was a limited period deal, but *two years*? Wasn't that a bit extreme?

'What's for breakfast?' Vatsala asked, re-entering the kitchen.

'You're ready already?' I asked, amazed. Didn't she leave the kitchen just seconds ago?

'Yep,' she said, stuffing her mouth with the omelette I had cooked. 'Is the toast done?'

'Almost. Did you take a shower?' I asked suspiciously.

'Yes, of course.'

'Vatsala . . .' I gave her a slightly fierce stare.

'What? Okay, fine. I did not take a shower. Big deal,' she shrugged.

'It is your first shoot. Take it seriously,' I chided. Although Vatsala was nineteen, it felt like she was . . . *four*. I sometimes felt like I was her mother.

'I don't get why taking a shower is so necessary. It is basically just a waste of time, soap and water!'

I thought about a way to respond to that but figured that— no, I was *not* supposed to reply to that. I turned to go to my room. Unlike Vatsala, I needed a shower.

'Don't take too much time, else we will get late for work. We can't trust these locals,' she called.

'Yeah, yeah,' I called back, as I picked up my clothes from the cupboard. As if she was the one living in Mumbai since the past two years. Brains like a baby and she acted so wise. This girl, I tell you.

～

'And cut,' the director said and everyone heaved a sigh of relief. Live sections of the shows are always the most dreaded ones.

'Good job,' a crew member said to Vatsala.

'Thanks,' she replied politely and made her way to where I stood and watched her first shoot. 'Was I okay?' she asked me.

'Yes, you were good,' I smiled at her.

'Really?'

'Yes, really. A little nervous, but good.'

'Was it visible? My nervousness?' she asked, looking worried.

'To me—yeah. But it won't be to the viewers, I'm sure. So, relax,' I said.

She turned to look at the rest of the crew work efficiently in their respective departments. And I looked at her. She was pretty. Not essentially conventionally beautiful, but pretty. She had a warm, personable face. The kind of face that would look cute even if she chose to frown all the time. Which she usually did—frowning, tilting her chin up an extra inch, angry at the world in general. She was just a kid, in a big city, who was too stubborn to show that anything scared her. She always kept her exterior rude. If she thought that it would drive people away from her, she was hugely mistaken. Apart from the fake angry expression she had on her forever, everything about her invited people in.

I had known her for just fifteen days, but it felt like I had known her since ages. I knew what she really was—a sweet girl, afraid of trusting people and letting them in. I knew what she projected herself to be—aloof, arrogant, someone you would prefer staying away from.

'Do you like it here?' I asked.

'Yes. It was fun,' she replied. 'But, I am kind of worried . . . Will I look okay on screen?'

'Chill. You will be fine,' I smiled. 'You will not believe how bad my first shoot was. We had to re-do the whole thing because I looked so pathetic.'

'You're kidding me! You look so cool in all your advertisements. So flawless!'

'You will look flawless too. They will take care of that,' I assured her. 'People always look better on screen than they actually are.'

She studied my face and said, 'You look amazing off screen too.'

I smiled and shrugged. Somehow, even though I was a professional model and everything, compliments had a tendency to make me uncomfortable. It was mostly because I always felt that the other person was exaggerating. To get laid. Come on, it was Mumbai and I was a model.

'I'm straight!' Vatsala said and I realized I had said the last part aloud.

'Huh? Oh. I didn't mean *you*. Was just saying generally . . .' I said, embarrassed.

'Thank God. And just for the record—if I were a lesbian, I would go for a girl who is dark. And has her hair cropped short. Is at least four inches taller than me . . .'

'That is basically how guys look,' I pointed out.

'Exactly. I would never go for a girl.'

'Oh shit! What if I offer? It would be pretty convenient, you know? With us sharing a flat . . .'

She looked at me, thought for a minute and said, 'Get a tan, crop your hair and wear high heels. See you tonight.'

And that was the only sex talk I got that day. I prefer not to count *paan*-belching producers with paunches hanging over their crotches. And they say that modelling is a glamorous business.

Behind the Scenes

'Isn't this shorter than before?' I asked. I was referring to the costume we were supposed to wear for the shooting of a magazine advertisement. Somehow, I remembered it being longer when we had had our fittings. It was not the first time such a thing had happened.

'And tighter,' Allya agreed.

'Should we say something?'

'Are we in a position to?' she asked.

I thought about it for a moment. It was the biggest and highest paying contract we had landed in the last few months. And somehow, even though Allya was way taller and prettier than me, her career was even more on the rocks. It was really weird, because even though I considered myself reasonably appealing and had likeable facial features, I stood nowhere even close to Allya. She was the kind of girl that guys think about when they shag at night.

She had joined the fashion industry almost five years ago and had been an instant hit. She was one of those girls who are just *meant* for modelling. Three inches taller than me, she had the fairest and smoothest of skins, with the highest of cheekbones and eyes that would actually sparkle even without makeup. She even had the quintessential Angelina Jolie pout! She had ruled the ramps for two whole years, before deciding to take a break and enter the advertisement world.

And then, she had gone down. People said she had 'lost her touch' and she had proved them right. That 'break' from the ramp had cost her her career.

And of course, there was a guy involved. *There always is.*

The ghosts of the unprofessional way in which she had acted almost three years ago still haunted her career. She was just twenty-three, and although we never said it aloud, we both knew that her career was at its end. It would take nothing short of a miracle to save it. Or maybe sleeping around a bit.

My career was in a much better state. But when I was with her, I pretended that we were on the same boat. It was pretty difficult for me, considering that I was not a negative person at heart, but worrying about my career in front of her made her feel like she had a friend by her side. So whenever I was with her, I always took care to act as if my life was over too.

'You're right,' I said in a low voice. 'We can't do anything.'

'Gosh, I *so* hate this. I feel so humiliated,' she said.

'Me too,' I said, and I meant it. The outfits we were wearing were so short and tight that I was having trouble to walk and breathe.

'We should go. They are calling for us,' Allya said.

We went to the set and I looked around to see the arrangements. Apart from the two of us, there were three other models there, wearing equally disgusting outfits. Weren't we shooting for an advertisement of some electronics brand, to go into magazines and banners? Why do we have to be so scantily clad to meet that purpose, again?

When I saw the girls move, it looked so vulgar that I thanked God that it was a still-photo shoot. If I looked like that when I moved too, which I probably did, I would have died before letting the world see it on screen. Maybe that was the reason why my career never went beyond fairness creams. Because I was never much into the whole concept of *compromising*.

Soon, we started posing with all kinds of electronic devices and I hoped it would be over soon so I could go home. It felt like I was working in some porn movie—although my expression didn't show it, I was thinking about what I would cook for dinner while working.

The photographer was directing me to pose with a stereo system when one of the other models came to me and said, 'Mr Valli wants to see you.'

'Me? Now?' I asked, not sure if I had heard it right. Mr Valli was a partner at the electronics company we were shooting for that day. Why he would need to meet a model who was just advertising his brand was beyond me. Or maybe not . . . paan-belching bastard.

'Yes. He is in the green room,' she pointed her index finger towards it.

'Okay, thanks,' I said.

Allya met my eye from across the set and raised her eyebrow. I shrugged back.

'Mr Valli?' I called, standing outside the green room.

'Who is it?' came a voice from inside.

'Chhavi Mukharjee. You wanted to see me, sir?'

'Oh yes, Chhavi. Come on in. The door is open,' he said. His voice was suddenly very jolly. I instinctively became cautious.

'Yes, sir?' I asked after I let myself in. He, like all such people, was middle aged, pot-bellied, suit wearing man with a receding hairline and stained teeth. The ones who were always horny and groping. I had left the door slightly ajar and taken care to stand as close to it as possible, without making it very obvious. These people have big ego issues. Especially the really guilty ones.

'Chhavi . . . come in, come in. Sit,' he motioned to a couch in front of him. *So now there's a couch in the scene too. Perfect.*

'Actually, sir, I left the shoot in between. And I really need to get back to it. Was there something urgent you needed to talk to me about?'

'Oh yes, yes,' he said, nodding feverishly and motioning to the couch again. 'Have a cup of coffee with me. I am sure five minutes would not do any harm to the shoot.'

'Of course, sir,' I said and took a seat at the couch. Allya knew where I was. And at least there was a table separating the two of us, I thought.

'So, how are things going? You are struggling a little, I hear?'

Isn't every model? I thought. 'I'm doing okay, thank you,' I said with a tight smile.

'Well, that is really nice to hear,' he said and smiled at me.

I smiled back. Fake, of course. I could not make out exactly what he was getting at. Especially because he did *not* look at my fully revealed legs even once.

'Anyway, Chhavi, I have a business proposal for you. A proposal that would do wonders to your career.'

Shit.

'Why don't you come to this small party that we have at my place tonight?' he suggested.

Shit. Shit.

'Sure, sir,' I said, eager to leave the room. If you are a model and if you live in Mumbai, I will give you some free advice—do *not* go to 'small' parties organized at a rich man's 'place' ever. For these people, real parties are never 'small' and are never organized at someone's 'place'. So, if you do make the mistake of going, you might end up being the only guest in their 'party'.

Been there. Done that.

'Brilliant! I would love to introduce you to my family—'

'That would be great, sir,' I said and got up to leave.

'Chhavi, wait!' he called from behind. 'You would enjoy meeting my son. He is very keen on you . . .'

'Oh?' I paused. So this is what he was getting at? I had actually started to feel somewhat offended that his eyes had not once wandered to my breasts yet. It almost felt like he wanted me just for the actual intercourse. No foreplay. And that is hugely insulting.

Now it made sense; he wanted me for sex, yes. But not for himself. *For his son!*

'Yes, he is quite a charming guy . . .'

'I am sure he is, sir,' I said, emphasising the *sir*, in a mocking tone. I was outside the door by then.

'Why are you in such a rush?' he asked and a few people turned to look at us.

'I have to go back to the shoot, *sir*, I have kept them waiting long enough, don't you think?'

'Oh, they won't mind. They know that you are with me.'

'Exactly,' I said and looked away.

'What does that mean?'

'Nothing,' I said, softly this time. I *so* did not want to create a scene.

'*You fucking slut!*' he suddenly thundered and everybody turned to look at us. 'Are you saying that I was molesting you? Tell me. Are you implying that—?'

'I am not implying anything, *sir*. Let me go back to work and—'

'Did I even so much as *look* at you? Did I—'

'I never said that,' I said.

'Then? What *did* you say?'

'You are creating a scene for no reason, sir.'

'Oh yeah? Now a roadside whore will tell me what is reason enough to——?'

'Mind your language, Mr Valli,' a firm, male voice intervened. I turned to look and saw a guy in his early twenties come to stand next to me.

Valli looked appalled. 'And who the hell are you to——?'

'That doesn't matter. Apologize,' he said sharply. I was still staring at him. He was a good six feet tall, and had an appealing lean frame. His face was partly hidden by a stubble, which implied that he had not shaved for three days. And his eyes had an unusual twinkle in them which made him look . . . alive. Yes, that was the perfect word to describe it—*alive*. Overall—I grudgingly agreed—that my saviour was really hot.

'For what? For giving her an offer a million models would kill for?' Valli shot, turning to me.

'No, sir. That was really kind of you, actually . . . but maybe you could apologize for the invitation to the *small* party you are having at your *place* tonight?' I asked with the most sincere expression on my face.

'I, uh . . .' Valli instantly faltered. Two years in this industry is a long time. You could tell what meant what.

'Yes, sir? You said something?' I asked, louder.

'I just . . .'

'What?' I gave him a fierce stare. Somehow, now that I knew everyone on the set was watching us, I felt brave. A lot braver than I was a few minutes ago, alone with him in the green room. Or maybe it had something to do with the hot guy standing next to me, who had come to my rescue, in an utterly filmy way.

'I just wanted you to meet my family,' he said, looking around at people, nodding and expecting them to look convinced.

'Your *family?* You mean your *son?* The one who's quite charming and is very keen on me?' I asked innocently.

He pursed his lips.

'Thank you very much for the invite, Mr Valli. But, I think I am going to have to pass. I have a date with, umm . . . this guy tonight,' I said pointing at the hot guy standing next to me.

'Ohh . . . right.' The hot guy played along.

'Now if you'll excuse us, we have a photo shoot to wrap up?' I said.

Valli gave the slightest of nods.

'Let's go, honey?' I said and pulled the hot guy away from the rest of the crew.

'Whoa,' he said, once we were out of everyone's earshot. 'Quite a fighter, you are!'

I blushed instantly. 'You don't know these people. They are all—'

'I *do* know how things are. I have been in the industry for the last five years now,' he replied.

'You have? I'm so sorry, I don't know you . . .'

'Tushar Mehra,' he extended his hand. 'I am a photographer—'

'Ah yes! I have heard your name before. Aren't you the one who works for *Vogue?*' I asked.

'I used to. Presently going freelance.'

'Oh, great,' I said. Not exactly. In our industry, *freelance* is synonymous to *unemployed*. It's just a polite way of saying—*no one in the whole freaking world thinks that I am good enough to be hired on a permanent basis.*

As if reading my mind, he said, 'No, not *that* freelance. I am not bragging or anything, but I have been doing really well in my career recently and have quite a few offers in my hand at the moment.'

'Nice.'

'In fact, there is so much demand in the market for me, that I hardly get time to even—'

'Okay. So now it's getting close to bragging,' I cut him off, smiling.

'You can't blame me for trying to make a good impression on a girl as pretty as you, can you?' He smiled back.

'And now you are flirting too.'

'Forgive me if I am a little rusty. Haven't needed to flirt with a girl since a long time. Usually, they—'

'—fall all over you, don't they?' I ask.

'More or less, yeah,' he shrugged nonchalantly.

'You are *so* full of yourself,' I said and turned to leave. I had had enough for a day. There was no way I was going to go through the full shoot. And I was still wearing my slut outfit, I suddenly remembered.

'*Naah!* I just act that way. I read somewhere that girls dig bad guys. But that doesn't work for you, I guess?'

'I am afraid not,' I said and walked away.

'Hey, wait!' he said, walking up to me. 'Where are you going?'

'To change.'

He looked at me from hair to toenails, and it gave me chills. He seemed to be lost for a moment, but gathered himself up pretty neatly. He cleared his throat and asked, 'And, after that?'

'Home.'

'But then, what about our date?'

'What date?' I asked.

'The one you told Valli about?'

We had reached the changing room by then. I smiled at him and opened the door to enter.

'At least tell me your name . . .' he said.

I thought for a second. Remember the movies in which the heroine doesn't tell the guy her name and he has to struggle to find out? I wanted to do this that way. Or maybe to say

Shashikala or Pushpa or something. But on second thought I changed my mind—no, it might stick. Imagine him calling me Shashikala every time we met. No way!

'No,' I replied.

'What? Why? Oh, come on!' Tushar seemed baffled.

I shook my head, smiled sweetly at him and shut the door on his face, leaving him outside.

Hammered and Stoned

I motioned the bartender for a refill. Gosh, after the dreadful day I had, I *so* needed to drink. If what happened earlier that day was not enough, on my way back home, I got a call from the firm I had to shoot with next week. They said I won't be 'needed on the set' anymore. That was just a polite way they chose to ask me to *buzz off*. I had been expecting this, but not so soon. I knew Valli would not take the insult lying down. God knew what was going to follow. It wasn't like I had many offers, anyway. Pissing off a man like Valli wasn't such a good idea, I realized in retrospect.

I had got home to find a note by Vatsala saying that she would be spending the night with Ankit. Which didn't make sense to me. Didn't Ankit stay at a boys' hostel? Well, none of my business.

I had turned on my heel and made my way to the bar. I was in no mood to spend the night, locked up alone in my apartment. Especially since my liquor stock was non-existent at the moment. Actually, it was non-existent at all moments, because I am not essentially a regular drinker. But some things just call for getting sloshed. Like when I am sexually harassed. Or mentally screwed. So this time, drinking was well justified. *Hawaiian Shack* called out to me.

There is nothing better than alcohol and vanity to pull you out of a bad mood. So I had made a conscious effort to dress well to cheer myself up. I looked down at myself to check. I was wearing this really amazing deep red dress that I had got from D&G, and it had cost me a fortune, obviously. But it had been worth it. The way it complemented my figure, I tell you! I really was looking pretty hot that night, if I say so myself!

'Chhavi!' I heard someone call my name.

'Huh? Oh. Hi, Kaushal,' I said. Kaushal was a guy I had dated for a few months sometime last year, before it had become glaringly obvious that we both weren't really into each other. So we had broken up. Bad kisser, too.

'Long time, eh?' he smiled. He looked genuinely pleased to see me.

'Not since the breakup,' I replied evenly.

'Uh, yeah . . . umm, meet Sophie,' he said and motioned to a tall, dark girl with a horsey face standing next to him. 'My girlfriend.'

'Oh hey! It's so nice to meet you, Sophie,' I gave her a half hug. I think I was a little drunk. Tipsy, at least.

'Hi . . .'

'Chhavi,' I supplied.

'Chhavi,' Sophie said and turned to Kaushal. 'You have never mentioned her before?'

I sat back and observed their exchange, which soon turned heated. Possessive girlfriend, eh? And since she was not anorexic, I could guess that she was not a model. Rich dad, spoiled brat. Maybe Kaushal's career had not been going all that great. He actually had a pretty decent deal. Sophie wasn't fat or old, at least.

Will I have to go out with a rich, fat, mid-aged man when my career goes down? God no! I would prefer . . . umm, what would I prefer? Maybe it was time I had an alternate career option. My career wasn't going so well anymore and I didn't want to end up like Allya. I thought she had secretly started going to small parties. She did get herself a new bag. *Gucci.*

I definitely did not want to end up on that lane. I had to think of a good alternative plan. And this was a nice time to reflect; I actually think more clearly when I'm drunk, you see?

So, what options did I have? Should I just continue being cast in random brands of hair oil and washing powder that come my way? What is the future there—promotion to conditioners and washing machine?

Maybe I should make it big. Maybe I should try my luck in Miss India, win it, move on to Miss World and win it too. Propagating world peace? I could do that. And then again, Bollywood loves a beauty queen, doesn't it?

But wait! How tall do I need to be to contend for Miss India? And how tall am I, again? Darn. So, not Miss World and not an actress. What else am I good at? Singing? I guess not. If someone who sings as bad as Vatsala says I suck, I really must suck!

So, career-wise, I was doomed.

Maybe I should concentrate on enjoying life, instead. Idea—I should get a boyfriend and we should hire a Harley and go on a road-trip across the country. Brilliant. I have been saving ever since I came to Mumbai, it should be enough to make the trip, I was sure. *Get a boyfriend*—I made a mental note.

Or maybe I could turn all dark and evil. Killing innocent people just for the fun of it and never getting caught. In the end, when I do get caught, I would make newspaper headlines and everyone would know me. And dread me. Someone might even write my biography. And it will become an international bestseller and my name will become immortal in the pages of history.

Becoming a monk wasn't a bad option either. People would come to me, asking for my advice in all sorts of matters and I would go on helping everyone unconditionally and selflessly, until I decide to give up everything and relocate to the Himalayas and meditate forever. I could even give up eating and—

I was drunk.

'Hey! I thought you wouldn't come,' a voice interrupted my future planning.

I turned to look at the owner of the voice, to find a tall, handsome guy sitting on the adjacent stool. He was wearing a casual white T-shirt with a Spiderman graphic on it, teamed with washed out blue denims and awesome shoes. I *always* notice the shoes. After all, they define a person.

I studied his eyes—they were twinkling. His face was half-hidden beneath a slight stubble, giving him a rugged—and hot, for that matter—look. And then, I let my eyes rest on his lips for a while. He had Adrian Grenier lips. *Can this be Adrian?* I wondered. *No, you don't know him personally*, came a reply automatically. *And he doesn't know you exist.* Life wasn't worth living.

'Chhavi?' he said.

'Huh?' I stared blankly at the guy.

'You remember me?'

'Sure! You are . . .' I trailed. *Who was he?* And why did it feel like I had seen him before? And how come I didn't notice his lips when I saw him before?

'Tushar? From the shoot today?' He jolted my memory.

'Oh, right! Tushar, my saviour,' I sang. I shouldn't drink. Ever. 'Let's dance!' I held his arm and pulled him towards the dance floor.

'You're drunk,' he held me and said.

'Yes!' I replied, holding him close and swaying to the music.

'And, stoned?' he tilted my chin and studied my eyes.

'Yes!' I supplied again.

'Why?' he asked. He looked like he was planning to run away any minute.

'Had a very shitty day,' I said simply.

'So did I.'

'So are you drunk? Or stoned?'

'No, I am not,' he said.

'*Why?*'

'I was waiting for you!' he accused.

I laughed, clung to him and danced to the beats of the music booming into my ears. My body fit his perfectly. I was wearing a pair of four-inch high heels, and he was still a couple of inches taller than me. I liked that.

'Don't worry, I will do it all over again with you,' I said.

'I don't think you should drink anymore. And weed . . .' he said, looking concerned.

I looked up at him, flipped my hair back, tilted my head to the side and said, 'Is that what you say to a drunk girl?'

'I . . .'

'Why? Oh, you must be used to those pretty models from *Vogue*? Aren't you? So I don't cut it for you?'

'*Are you kidding me?* The whole bar is looking at you! You are *that* hot. Like, smoking,' he said, looking down at me. His eyes taking in every inch of my body, leisurely, yet hungrily.

I blushed. Somehow, even alcohol never helps my wariness at compliments. Why do I just *have to* blush and get all red in the face every time I am complimented? It gets so embarrassing, this Excessive Blushing Syndrome that I suffer from!

'What?' he asked. He looked amused at my reaction.

'You *meant* that,' I met his eye and said.

'Of course I meant that!'

'To get me to sleep with you?'

'No. Because that's the truth.' He looked angry.

'Oh . . . umm, actually, people usually say such things just to . . . you know? I'm so sorry. I didn't mean to offend you . . .'

He gave me half a smile, 'Too sweet, you are.'

'You're not mad?' I asked seriously. As serious as I could get, that is, given my drunken state.

'*Naah!* I was just kidding. Actually . . . I wouldn't really mind . . .' he trailed off.

'What?' I was struggling to keep up. All I could see was his lips moving. What they were saying never registered. Damn those sexy lips!

'Taking you to my place and . . . you know? I don't think I would mind that,' he winked.

I tore my eyes away from his lips to study his face. He was serious. I felt weak in the knees. 'You are too sober for that,' I said as I dragged him to the liquor counter. I wanted him to get drunk and . . . you know?

I Am Hungover You

'Mmm?' I spoke into my phone next morning.

'Chhavi?' the voice from the other side asked. Vatsala. I recognized her voice.

'Yes. What's up?' I asked, still not opening my eyes.

'Allya called. She has asked you to call her back. You were not receiving her calls?' she said.

'Hmm . . . I was sleeping.'

'I figured. Anyway, I'll be back home in an hour. Do you want me to get you something on the way?'

'Some milk,' I replied, opening my eyes. The ceiling did not look familiar. I frowned.

'Sure. Do you need anything else?' Vatsala asked.

'Where am I?' I wondered aloud.

'*What?*'

I turned on my side to see the hot guy from the previous day—Tushar—lying next to me on the bed. *Uh-oh.*

'Vatsala . . .'

'Chhavi? Hello? Hello? Hey, I cannot hear you—there is

22

too much traffic. If you want anything else, send me a text,' she said and hung up.

I sat up on the bed slowly, not taking my eyes away from Tushar even once. I paused for a minute, not moving, watching him sleep . . . trying to remember what had happened the previous night. Nothing came back.

My dress was missing. I turned around to look at him. He was lying on his back, the upper half of his body exposed. I could see the outline of his six-pack abs. Quite a sight, actually, but all I had on my mind in that minute was one question—did we pass out *before* or *after* making out?

I thought about what I should do. *Get up, get dressed and get out?* No, that would be so childish and chicken-ish. He would feel like I could not face him the morning after. So, I ruled away *getting out*. Though, *getting up* and *getting dressed* seemed like a good idea. So, I slowly picked up my clothes and made my way to the washroom. When I came back, I found Tushar exactly as I had left him. I looked around the room. Did we rent a hotel room last night? Obviously. How else did I end up here?

I could not believe I had actually done something like that. Yes, I had rented a motel room to make out with a guy once before. But that was different. It is different when you are in a relationship with the guy. But this . . . I was not someone who gets drunk and makes out with random strangers. To top that, I did not even remember exactly what I had done. I felt sluttish and was angry at myself for being so careless. I just *had to* know what had transpired the night before. If only to estimate exactly how horrified my parents would have been, had they known.

I walked to Tushar's side of the bed and sat down quietly. I touched his shoulder softly and said, 'Umm . . . Tushar? Wake up . . .'

'Hmm?' He opened his eyes almost instantly. I was a bit taken aback.

'I, uh, good morning,' I said sheepishly.

'Chhavi!' he said, sitting up on the bed.

'Erm, yeah. Hi,' I smiled. I didn't know what else to do.

He seemed too shocked to say anything. For a short while, he just kept staring at me. It made me nervous.

'Tushar, I . . . what happened last night? I mean—did we . . . you know . . .?'

He looked at me for a moment longer and said, 'You don't remember either?'

I shook my head. 'You don't too?'

'Not after we got here,' he said, looking around the room.

'Okay. But what do you remember? How did we get here?' I asked.

'You asked me to take you to my room.'

'Why do you have a room reserved in a hotel?'

'I don't live here, in Mumbai. I am here for business,' he explained.

'So where do you live?'

'Nowhere. I mean—I do not have a permanent residence. I just move around, you know, to wherever work calls.'

We kept silent for a while, our thoughts back to the previous night. I had asked him to take me back to his room. *Imagine.* I had actually had a one night stand. It felt strange; I had never expected to see myself in one of those. I needed to know more. 'So, what happened before we got here?' I asked evenly. 'All I remember is that we were dancing . . .'

'Right. We were dancing, and then you asked me if you were looking hot,' he said.

'I did that?' I asked, surprised.

'Yeah. And then you asked if I wanted to get into your pants.'

'Really? And what did you say to that?'

'That I wouldn't mind,' he answered with a lopsided grin on his face.

'Pervert.'

'What? You would have preferred it had I said *no?*'

I thought for a moment. Saying *no* would have implied that he found me undesirable. And that would have been a direct insult to me. 'I guess not,' I accepted grudgingly.

He smiled. 'After that, you forced me to drink and smoke weed with—'

'Forced?' I asked, looking pointedly at his body. A guy six feet tall was *forced* into drinking, against his will, by a near-anorexic model. Ha!

'Okay, I agree that I *did* co-operate a little,' he said. 'So, I got drunk, you got drunker. I got stoned, you got even more stoned. And the rest is history.'

'Did we have sex?' I asked, trying not to freak out.

'I don't know. I am still in my boxers . . . so,' he said.

'I saw.'

'You *saw?*'

'I mean—I checked.' I said.

'*Checked?*'

'Whatever, Tushar.'

'Darn. Why didn't I wake up before you? *I* should have been the one doing the checking,' he said and made an expression of immense loss. I felt nice. But why? He wanted to see me naked. What was there to feel good about?

'Flirt,' I said. And maybe blushed too.

'Not really. I'm not a flirt. But, I don't know why I always do that when I am with you.'

'I guess I should feel honoured?' I smiled.

'Ah, yes. You definitely should.'

'Sure. Now, back to the topic—*did* we or did we *not?*'

'What if we *did?* And what if we did *not?*' he asked.

'In both cases—I would prefer to know,' I said.

'See, if you are disappointed that we did *not*, we can do it now. I really do not have an issue,' he smiled wickedly.

'That is *so* generous of you! But—no, thanks. I think I'll pass. I'm not drunk. Or stoned.'

'You're mean.'

His fake-hurt expression was super-cute. I laughed and he joined in. But soon, a thought crossed my mind and wiped away the smile. 'Tushar, is this your wallet?'

'Yes, why? You're not going to *charge* me for last night, are you? Not done! We are not even sure we actually did it,' he teased.

'Be serious. Do you remember how many condoms you had in it before last night?' I asked.

'Yeah. Four,' he said.

'*Four*? Why?' It came out before I could stop it.

'Umm . . . for *sex*, maybe?' he mocked.

'Of course,' I got a little red in the face. 'Anyway. How many do you have now?'

'Four,' he checked and said, 'Oh, so if we did have sex, we did it without protection.' I met his eyes.

'I'm clean,' he said.

'That's not what I meant!'

'So . . . you . . . er . . . you have something?' he asked, suddenly looking very anxious.

'No! I definitely do *not* have something.' I laughed at his expression. He looked so worried that I wanted to go kiss him.

'Phew! For a moment there, you got me worried . . .' he sighed in relief.

I shook my head. 'No, what I meant was—what if I get pregnant?'

'You can get an i-pill. Just to be sure . . .'

'Uh. Right.'

We stared at each other, having no idea what to say next. 'Well, I should get going now . . .' I said.

'Umm . . . you want to go downstairs to grab a bite, first?'

'Oh, no thanks. I am okay.' I collected my things and he walked me to the door. 'Goodbye, then,' I said.

'I, uh, can I have your number?' he asked. For the first time since I had met him, he seemed a little shy, almost like a schoolboy. And it was immensely cute. I tried hard to keep my smile in check. I should act mysterious, I knew. Guys like that. But, come on! *Look at him.* He was definitely one of the handsomest guys around. And he was asking for *my* number.

'Why?' I looked up at him and asked innocently.

'Maybe we can meet up sometime . . .'

'Oh? Why don't you find it out the way you found out my name yesterday?'

He looked at me and nodded slightly, a slow smile creeping up on his face. 'If that's how you want it to be.'

I smiled and turned to leave.

'And Chhavi?'

'Yes?' I turned back to face him.

He suddenly pulled me towards him by the waist and kissed me softly on the mouth. The kind of sweet, too-short kiss that leaves you craving for more. I was shocked at first, since I had not seen it coming. I was caught off guard. And by the time I realized what was happening, it was already over. I wanted more . . . so much more!

'Just in case I didn't get a chance to do this last night,' he said.

I blushed and turned away to leave, wordlessly. I was in no condition to speak. All I had on my mind at that moment was one thought—*I should have been in my senses last night. It would have been so much better.*

~

'Hello?' I said to Vatsala on the phone for the second time that day.

'Where are you?' she asked.

'On my way home. You won't believe what happened, Vatsala. I spent the night with a random guy. A *hot* random guy. I got drunk last night and asked him to take me to his hotel room. Can you imagine?'

'No, I cannot imagine! Really?' I could feel her surprise. 'Did you guys *do it*?'

'Yeah, I think. Which reminds me, I should get an i-pill.' I looked around for a pharmacy store.

'What do you mean you *think* you did it? And i-pill? You didn't even use protection?'

'I don't remember. I was drunk. I ain't sure we even had sex, for the matter.'

'Chhavi, are you crazy? How can you be so freaking irresponsible?' Vatsala said and I instantly regretted telling her all that over the phone. It would have been fun to look at her face when she acted like a responsible adult, for a change.

'Chill. Let me come home first. And then you can shout at me all you want,' I said.

'Fine. I will wait,' she said and hung up.

All the way back home, I was smiling. I agree that it was all messed up and everything, but it was fun nonetheless. Waking up at a hot stranger's place, almost-naked, lying next to him . . . trying to figure out whether or not we had sex the previous night . . . it was something I had seen only in movies and happen to people around me.

I wondered why I didn't feel guilty about what happened, or did not happen. Maybe I was turning into one of those bad girls. Or maybe it was because I had started to like Tushar. Just maybe.

Take Me on a
Cool Road Trip!

'You have 2437 friends on Facebook,' I observed, sitting next to Vatsala, as she glared at her laptop. 'How?'

'Because I accept friend requests when people send them.'

'You accept *all* the requests you get?'

'No. Less than half,' she answered.

'And on what basis do you confirm or ignore?'

'I check their profile info. The music they listen to and the books they have read.'

'You view profiles of every person who sends you a request?' I asked.

'Yeah, most times. Though, if we have more than thirty mutual friends, I accept without checking,' she said seriously.

'So that's what you do on FB all day.'

'I have nothing else to do,' she shrugged.

If you are wondering why Vatsala got so many friend requests, I will tell you why. First—she was pretty. Second—she once wrote a book (some rubbish about a girl falling in love with a VJ on Facebook). And third—she was on TV once every week. She had a small fan following of her own. And she was just nineteen! Sometimes, it felt like she was a godsent to make me feel inferior.

'Is there a special reason for which you accept requests?'

'Yes. That's what Ronit used to do,' she said simply.

Ronit. Ronit Oberoi. The guy Vatsala wrote that book— *Love @ Facebook*—about. The VJ she fell in love with. She was so obsessed with him once, that she couldn't even think about any other guy. She would compare every guy that would cross her way to Ronit and somehow, Ronit ended up being better than every single one of them in her eyes. No one even came close. She would stalk him on FB and imagine that she meant something to him. Which, obviously, was *not* true. For him, she was just another crazy fan, who would never leave him alone and kept irritating him with senseless messages. Only, she didn't realize so.

When she finally did realize, she wrote a book about it! Which was the only good thing that came out of that obsession. She had been incredibly lucky to have had Ankit by her side when she got back to her senses. He had been in love with her since forever and was there when she closed Ronit's chapter of her life. She had finally been able to get over Ronit and move on.

Though, if you ask me, I really don't understand why it was so damn difficult. Yes, Ronit was pretty hot, with that adorable gash on one of his cheeks and that air of authority he seemed to carry around with him. But apart from that dimple and the . . . okay, stop. *Let's not lie.* To be fair to him—he was typical tall, dark, handsome kind. Some serious, dangerous hot stuff. But, face it—he was a celebrity. What were the odds that he would have noticed Vatsala and they would have shared something special?

'Ronit added friends, so you decided to do the same?'

'Right.'

'So, how are things going with Ankit?' I asked to change the topic.

'Awesome!' Vatsala's face lit up suddenly.

I smiled, sensing something *more* in the *awesome*. 'So, do you want to tell me about it?'

'Umm . . . we made out . . .' she turned away from the laptop to face me and said.

'So? Haven't you been doing that since the last six months?'

'Uh, yeah . . .' she blushed and looked away. 'What I meant was, we . . . you know . . .?'

'What?' I acted innocent, although I had a pretty good idea what she meant. It is not very often that I got to see Vatsala blush, and I wanted it to last as long as possible.

'I mean . . . we went *all the way*,' she said, blushing terribly by then.

'*All the way?*'

'Chhavi! You know what I mean.'

I laughed. 'Of course! I was just having fun. So? How was it?'

'It was, um, okay, I guess . . .'

'Just *okay*?'

'Yeah.' She shrugged her shoulders.

I had never seen a girl be so nonchalant about the first lovemaking of her life. And Vatsala, at that. The same girl who had been blushing so badly just seconds ago?

'Are you kidding me?' I said, shocked.

'Yes, I am kidding you! It was amazing. *Amazing.* That is the only word which can describe how I felt. Amazing.' She looked very adorable, with her eyes all bright and her face split into a wide smile. I suddenly realized exactly how much she loved Ankit. A lot more than she thought she did, at least.

'It didn't hurt?' I asked. My first time did. A lot. Mostly because the word *slow* never figured in the guy's dictionary.

'No. Not much. Just a little in the beginning. I was so scared at first . . .' she trailed away, staring at nothing, with a smile on her face.

I knew she was remembering it. I smiled. And I accept—I was a little jealous.

~

Later, when I had finally let her go to sleep, after coaxing every minute detail of her make out with Ankit, I sat alone in my bed, wondering. What were the chances that I would get someone like Ankit in my life? Someone who would love me selflessly, care for me unconditionally, look so sexy and take me on a road trip around the country?

Here, I should make it clear—Ankit was *not* taking Vatsala on a road trip. It was just that I would have liked to have a boyfriend who would take me on one. Imagine—I sitting behind him on a Harley, holding him, wearing my Ray Bans, with the wind blowing my long hair behind me . . .

My rather wishful thoughts were disturbed by my phone ringing. Who would call me at 1 a.m.?

'Hello?'

'Hey, Chhavi,' said a voice from the other end of the phone. 'Tushar.'

'Oh.'

'From the bar that night, remember? The photographer?' he tried to jolt my memory.

I laughed. 'Of course I remember you! I'm not drunk tonight.'

'Right. I thought you didn't remember . . .'

As if he was someone a girl could ever forget. Especially after seeing those six packs he hid under his T-shirts. And that goodbye kiss. Oh man, the kiss . . . 'I remember. So—I see you got my number.'

'Yeah. Piece of cake,' he said, proudly. 'How difficult can it be for a photographer to arrange a model's number?'

'Point,' I smiled.

'Hmm . . . so? What's up?'

I did not know how to answer that. Do I tell him that I had been sitting on my bed in the middle of the night, wondering where I would find a guy who would drive me around the country? And that I had been deciding the colour and design of the helmet I would wear on the much anticipated road trip? Actually, the *what's up* question is always such a pain. You usually do *not* do things that are interesting enough to be told to someone over phone. So you inevitably end up saying *nothing much*. Which was what I did then.

'Nothing much. Just going to sleep.' After all, that's what single girls do at night, right? Normal single girls, I mean. Ahem.

'Oh. You were about to sleep? I'm sorry. I didn't mean to disturb you . . .'

'No, no. It's not like that. I probably wouldn't have slept so early anyway,' I tried to repair the damage. If a guy calls you at night and you say you were going to sleep, it sends a crystal clear signal: *buzz-off*. I cursed myself for not thinking about that before.

'But you just said that you were going to sleep.'

'Umm . . . yeah, but . . .' Oh, man. This was getting awkward.

'But?'

'But that was because I didn't have anything better to do,' I said.

'And this is better?' he fished.

Well, truth be told—*nothing* is better than sleeping. But then again, this could be a close second. 'Are you kidding me? This is *way* better than sleeping!' I lied easily.

'That's nice to know.' I could feel him smile at the other end.

Again, I had no idea what to say. And he, apparently, was having the same problem. I asked if there was a special reason for which he called me and he said he just wanted me to know that he had my number. So, after that, having nothing to talk about, we hung up.

Though I didn't want to.

And I think he didn't want to, either.

As I switched off the bedside lamp and rolled over to sleep, I wondered—*if I dated him someday, would he take me on a cool road trip?*

The New Offer

The doorbell chimed and I went to get it. It was Ankit. And as always, he was looking immensely cute. *Vatsala is a lucky girl*—is inevitably the first thought that crosses my mind whenever I see Ankit. And that day was no different.

'Hi,' he said.

'Hey! Come on in,' I said and moved to let him in.

'How is everything?'

'Good. Nothing great, though,' I motioned him to sit.

'Having troubles with the contracts?'

'Yeah. Just that, the only trouble is that I'm not getting any,' I said sadly. 'Had a tiff with the producer of an ad film. He made sure I don't get any other assignments.'

'He can do that? And you can't do anything about it?'

'Not really. I'm just a model. Who would care? And of course—he's rich.'

'Can I do something to help?'

'*Naah!* It will be okay. I'm sure it's just temporary.' At least I hoped so.

'Best of luck,' he said. 'Where's Vatsala?'

'In the shower,' I said.

'Really?' he asked and I laughed at his expression.

'Yes, *really*. And she is going to do that a lot more often. I am going to take care of it,' I announced. It would be easy, really. I would just have to keep reminding her that now that she was physically involved with Ankit, she couldn't possibly continue with her anti-bathing lifestyle. And since their relationship was still in the honeymoon phase, she would take every pain to impress Ankit, I was sure.

'Well, good luck with that,' Ankit laughed.

'You're here!' Vatsala said, coming into the living room.

'Hey,' Ankit got up to hug her.

'You're looking hot,' Vatsala said seriously, getting out of his embrace to observe him.

'So are you,' he replied.

'No, you're *really* looking hot,' she said, turning to me to ask, 'Isn't he looking hot?'

'Absolutely.' I met Ankit's eye and winked. If there was someone who had more trouble dealing with compliments than me, it was him. And Vatsala looked so sincere that it almost made me laugh.

Soon, they left for the day, leaving me alone. Which was a good thing, as looking at them together, I could not help myself from imagining them in bed. I know it sounds kind of pervert-ish, but that is how it has always been with me. If a guy introduces his girl to me, my mind immediately starts imagining them together in bed. Weddings are especially hard for me.

Ever since I had first met them, I had imagined Ankit and Vatsala to be highly compatible physically. And since now I knew exactly how great they were together, with *every minute detail*, the picture that came up into my mind on seeing them with each other that morning was very vivid. Very.

It was a good thing they left before reading my mind. It would have been so embarrassing otherwise.

I turned on my laptop, with a plan to watch *Entourage* all day. Ankit was going to drop Vatsala to her shoot after their date. So I knew that she would not be back till the night. Spending the day with Adrian seemed like a good idea.

I was halfway through my eighth consecutive episode of the day when the doorbell rang. It was Allya.

'Hi. What's up?' she looked around the apartment and asked.

'Nothing much,' I gave my patent reply. 'Just watching something on the laptop.' I didn't say *Entourage*. She was a *Gossip Girl* and *90210* type of a girl. *Desperate Housewives* even, I doubted. So, she would never get it. We were on *way* different wavelengths on this matter.

'Hmm. You have something to drink?' she asked unnecessarily, since she was already peering into the refrigerator.

'Beer, I guess,' I replied, unnecessarily too, as she had already taken out a can and was in the process of opening it. Allya was by far the one of the heaviest drinkers I had ever known. She had her reasons.

'You want one?'

'No, thanks,' I replied.

She flopped on the couch and announced, 'I've got some good news!'

'What?' I asked, excited. New assignment? For me? For her? Honestly, I would feel equally happy if it was for her. She needed it more than I did.

'I got an offer . . . for *both of us* in a television ad.'

'Oh wow! That's great! What is the ad for?'

'Condoms,' she said simply.

'Sorry?'

'Yeah, you heard it right. Condoms.'

'I . . .' I couldn't think of anything to say. *Is this some kind of a joke? We got an offer to be cast in a condom advertisement? And Allya is actually excited about it? Has she totally lost her mind?*

'So, are you in?'

'Allya . . .' I tried to think of something to say. The expression on her face scared me. She looked so aloof. So detached. As if she didn't care about a thing in the world.

'See Chhavi, all we have to do is dress up and stand there in front of the camera for ten seconds. We're not the leads. We don't even have a dialogue.'

'But, it's—'

'I know. But's it's not that bad. Think coherently—it's absolutely zero work and easy money.'

'Still . . .' I could not imagine myself being cast in a condom ad. Not that I tried very hard to imagine, though. And that was because I didn't want to. I wasn't in *that* bad a condition.

'I'm taking it. Think about it. You don't have any other option.'

'At the moment, yes, I do not have any other option. But I will. Something will come up,' I said, more to convince myself than her.

'*When?* Oh, come on, Chhavi! Don't be foolish. Take this offer when it is still on the table.'

'Allya, I can't.'

'Why? It's hardly porn! It's just another bloody advertisement. Hell, you will have more clothes on your body than you had on the Valli shoot.'

I knew what she was saying was the truth. And I knew it was probably a mistake to pass that offer, mostly because no one would even notice us, standing somewhere in the background. But advertising for a condom brand did *not* sound good to me. It felt almost insulting. Degrading. Maybe Allya's career needed such desperate measures. Mine certainly did not. Not yet, at least.

'Chhavi, trust me—take it.'

'I can't.' I shook my head.

'Okay then. Your loss,' she shrugged.

I did not know what got into Allya that day. She was not usually *that* negative. But that day, the way she was acting was actually scary. I knew that my own career was at a much better position than hers, but seeing her like that gave me the chills. *Two years down the line, will I become like that too?*

Maybe it was time I did something serious about my modelling career.

I thought about it all day and decided—it was high time I hired an agent. I needed someone who would take care that I had offers on my table regularly. I knew a good chunk of money from my pay cheques would go to him, but I was okay with sharing my pay. It was better than receiving zero pay, at least.

I searched for good agents available in Mumbai on Google and *loads* of them came up in the search. I had no clue what to do, who to go to.

Then I remembered Tara. She was a model too and I had worked with her on some projects a few times in the past couple of years. And I knew for a fact that she had an agent. I remembered her mentioning something about it. I dialled her number.

'Hello?' she answered.

'Hey. Is this Tara?'

'Yeah. Who is this?'

'Chhavi Mukharjee. You remember me?' I asked.

'Umm, Chhavi . . . of course! Say. What's up?'

'Nothing much. You're doing fine?'

'Yeah, I'm good. So? How did you remember me?' she asked.

'Actually, I was looking for an agent. Could you suggest someone I should go for?'

'Oh, yes. Naitik Mittal. He was my agent. Real gem. You can trust him blindly!'

'*Was?*' I asked. *If she fired him, why should I hire him?*

'Yeah. I gave up modelling. Didn't you hear?'

'Umm, no. I haven't really been in the loop recently. Why are you leaving, though?'

'I am engaged. I am getting married!' I could hear the excitement in her voice.

'Ooh! Congratulations! That's great news!' I cheered, genuinely happy for her. Even though I had met her just a few times, I had always thought she was not meant for the modelling industry. She used to look so *lost* sometimes, like a twelve-year-old at a big carnival.

'Thank you. I'm so happy,' she said. I could almost see her million-watt smile in her voice.

'So, who's the lucky guy?'

'Oh, you don't know him. Parth Shrivastav. He's not from this industry. We met at a party through mutual friends. And I *so* love him.'

'Sounds amazing!' I smiled.

'Listen, you just *have to* come to the wedding. It is in Mumbai, so you do not have an excuse. And bring someone with you.'

'Oh, okay. I would love to come.' *And see what your to-be-husband looks like. And what you guys would be like together. In bed.*

'I will mail you an official invite. And I will also mail you Naitik's contact. Take my word, hire him. You will never find an agent as awesome as him.'

I let out a sigh of relief.

The Vivid Picture

Naitik Mittal seemed like quite a character. He was a dynamic guy in his mid-thirties. He worked for an agency that had around fifty other such agents. But within two minutes of entering the agency, it was clear to me that amongst them all, he was the most hated one. I liked him instantly.

The reason he was so universally hated at his agency and the entire industry was that he never watched his mouth. Or actions. Once he took up a client, he would do *anything* and *everything* to make sure that awesome offers kept flowing. He knew everyone worth knowing and knew everyone's every dirty secret. He never thought twice before using it to his advantage.

More than often, his ways were questioned and his language was frowned upon. Over the years that he had spent in the industry, he had developed quite a few enemies. But that did not shake his credibility in the least. His clients never saw a bad day and his pictures kept maintaining a permanent residence on several people's dart-boards.

He was the kind of guy you wouldn't want to be on the wrong side of. But once he was on your side, you could rest assured that you would be well taken care of. Nothing could touch you. *Nothing*.

He would make you a star.

The only thing worrying me was—he chose his clients carefully. Very, *very* carefully. Tara told me that it had taken him seven phone calls from four different, extremely influential people to get her the first appointment with him. And after that, he had grilled her and made her sweat for seven entire months before finally agreeing to take her up.

I did not have that kind of time. If things kept going the way they were, in seven months, my career would dead. But at least he had agreed to meet me. All it had taken was one short phone call from Tara. I told you—he took good care of his clients. Ex or otherwise.

'Mr Mittal will see you now,' his assistant came to me and said. She looked better than me and her dress must have been ten times costlier than mine. Obviously, I was extremely intimidated.

She guided me to his office, knocked on the door twice and opened it. 'Ms Chhavi Mukharjee is here to see you, Naitik,' she announced and left.

I got into the office and looked around. I was impressed. The place stank of money. And it was *huge*. Like enormous. At least twice the size of the apartment I shared with Vatsala. An entire corner was devoted to a casual sitting area, complete with three huge bright red couches, arranged over the plush cream carpet covering the length of the room. One face of the wall was replaced completely with glass, which gave an amazing view of the city.

Another corner had a compact bar, complete with a wide range of liquor arranged on the shelves, and bar stools surrounded the counter. The entire corner was decorated in silver and grey, clearly separating the bar from the rest of the office, just not physically.

But what caught my attention was the man sitting behind the large teakwood desk, which was shining more brightly than a brand new Porsche. I looked at Naitik, dressed impeccably in a sharply cut midnight blue suit, staring intently at his iMac's screen. As agents go, he was by far the best-looking I had seen.

He looked ruthless. His jawline shouted *no-mercy*. But as soon as I put my eyes on him, I decided to like him. Until he opened his mouth, that is.

'Hi . . .' I said meekly.

'Chhavi Mukharjee. You are here why?' he shot, still staring at his computer.

'I, uh . . .' I had no idea how to react. *No pleasantries?*

'You're wasting my time. Speak. Or get the fuck out.'

'I'm here because . . . umm . . . Tara must have told you about me?' He was so dominating that I applauded myself for being able to deliver a full sentence in front of him.

'Which is obvious. How else do you think your pretty ass got entry into my office?'

'Mr Mittal, I—'

'*What?* Lily!' he suddenly roared, cutting me off.

'Yes, Naitik?' his assistant was there in a breath.

'Would you be kind enough to guide Ms Chhavi Mukharjee out of my office and help her find her tongue back?'

Lily stared at him. So did I.

'*Now!*' he shouted.

'Ms Mukharjee, please . . .' Lily turned to me with a scared expression on her face. *What? They are throwing me out?* Just like that? Because I wasted about five seconds of his *precious* time? I had to do something. He was my only hope.

'Mr Mittal . . .?'

'*What?*' he barked, and looked at me properly for the first time since I had entered the office.

'I would like you to represent me,' I said, and put up a show of confidence.

'Oh yeah? You would? And why the fuck do you think I would agree to take you?'

'Because I am good at what I do.'

'And what *do* you do?' he spat.

'I am a model.'

'Really? A bloody dwarf like you? What are you? 4'1"?' he asked, his eyes travelling the length of my body.

'5'5".'

'Same thing. Both mean *"no entry"* in the modelling industry. So get the fuck out of my head.'

'I am a print model,' I said, as I tried to stay calm.

'So why did you not say so in the first place? Has someone *paid* you for wasting my time and pissing me off?'

'Mr Mittal, I—'

'*Would you fucking stop calling me that already?*' he suddenly bellowed.

'But what else do I call you then? Isn't that your name?'

'No. That's my *surname*. *Name* is what comes *after* the "Mr" and *before* the "Mittal",' he mocked, dramatically, emphasising words to make me feel stupid.

'Okay. Naitik, then. Naitik, I am here because I need you to be my agent.'

'Why? Are you having trouble making a living, babes?'

'It's getting kind of—' I started to explain but he cut me off.

'But you said you were good at what you do? So if you're so good at it, why do you need me?'

'Because I am good at *modelling*, not fetching offers.'

'If you are good enough, offers find you. You do not have to go *fetch* them, as you put it,' he said.

'That has stopped happening now—'

'Why? Lost your charm, have you? And you thought I would keep your little boat floating? Well, you were badly mistaken. *Fuck off.*'

'*What?*' I said. I was taken aback.

'Get the fuck out of here. Out of my office, out of my building. *Out!*' he shouted.

I stood there staring at him, trying to comprehend what just happened. Was that some kind of a stupid test? Or was he just plain retarded?

'What are you still doing here? What part of "out" did your pretty head find difficult to comprehend?' he looked up at me and asked.

'I am sure you must have heard this before plenty of times, but I will repeat it anyway—*you are an asshole,*' I said before I turned to leave. If that was what Tara went through for four months before he took her up, I would prefer selling peanuts for a living.

'And you are mine, babes,' he called from behind.

'*Excuse me?*' I spun around. 'What do you mean I am *yours?*'

'Yes—mine. My *client,* I mean. I would not mind you being *mine* otherwise too, though.'

I looked at him, trying to read his face. He is ready to represent me? Is this some kind of a joke?

'Why the million dollar expression?' he asked.

'Are you kidding me?'

'No. I have the most serious fucking expression on my face. Do I look like I am bloody kidding?'

'So you are serious about representing me? And why is that?' I asked.

'Because you are good at what you do.'

'What *do* I do? Dwarf modelling at the pathetic height of 4'1" that I have?'

'Oh! So now that I decide to take you up, the table turns? You can bombard me with nonsensical questions?' he asked.

'No, I am serious. Why are you taking me up? Have you even seen any of my work?'

'Of course. Why else did I agree to see you then?'

'Because Tara called?' I suggested.

'There was a difference of ten minutes, babes. *After* Tara called and *before* I agreed to see you.'

'Ten minutes were enough?'

'Ten seconds were enough,' he said.

'So why did you waste the other nine minutes, fifty seconds?'

'I was thanking my stars for getting me you!'

'I . . .' I trailed off, not knowing how to react. He was a strange person. Everything I had heard about him was true. Smart, arrogant, cocky bastard. A lean-mean machine. But he was willing to take me up as a client.

He was willing to take me up as a client!

Naitik Mittal thought I still had it in me. He thought that I was good enough to be his client. And I got him in just one meeting. It was just too good to be true. I could not find words to describe what I was feeling then.

He got up to shake my hand. 'Welcome aboard. Let's kick some serious ass.'

~

'Vatsala, where are you?' I asked her over phone that evening.

'I am on my way back home. Be there in five.'

By the time Vatsala got there, I was ready. We just *had* to go out that night. It had been over a month that Vatsala had come to Mumbai and we had been sharing an apartment. And we were still to go out together. Life had been so busy . . . for her, that is. With the new job and the awesome boyfriend. I, on the other hand, was usually just finding ways to pass my time.

But now that I had this kickass agent finding work for me, I was not going to have so much free time anymore, was I?

'Are you going somewhere?' Vatsala asked, as she entered the apartment. 'You look good, by the way.'

'Thanks. And you are coming with me. We're partying tonight.'

'Why are we having a party suddenly? Any special reason? Is it your birthday today?'

'No. Just shut up and get dressed,' I said.

Music boomed in our ears as we entered Poison. Even though Vatsala had been completely against going out that night, I had been successful in convincing her. It had become infinitely easier when I had called Ankit and invited him to join us.

'I do *not* like this,' Vatsala said, clutching my tiny finger.

'You do not like *what?*' I asked, looking around. The crowd looked pretty decent and the music was superb. What was there to *not* like?

'This. This place. People are *dancing* here,' she said, as if dancing was a novel concept in her eyes.

'Yes, they are. That is exactly what people do at discos.'

'That is why I do *not* like discos. I hate this! Chhavi, I do not dance. *I cannot dance!*' She was pulling my tiny finger so hard, that it was in danger of getting ripped off my hand.

'Relax. You don't have to. It is not a compulsion. We will just sit and drink.' I almost laughed aloud at the expression of sheer terror on her face.

'I do not drink, either. I had planned to start once I got out of home but now it doesn't appeal to me in the least,' she said and made a face.

'Never mind. Just sit back and enjoy the music. Ankit must be on his way. Andheri is not all that far away from here.'

As I sat there and sipped my wine, Vatsala gave me details about every new song the DJ played. She was a music freak. She knew every single song in the world. It was creepy. And she didn't dance. That was even creepier. She was just nineteen! How could she *not* dance?

'Where is Ankit?' she asked after some time.

'Must be here any moment,' I replied, looking around. It wasn't Ankit's face I saw. 'Tushar?' I wondered aloud.

'Huh?' Vatsala asked, as she looked around at the direction I was staring at. 'You know him?'

At that moment, Tushar spotted me across the floor and made his way towards us. He was dressed in all-black that night and still had that slight stubble on his face. He was looking exceptionally sexy. My heart skipped a beat.

'Are you stalking me?' he asked angrily, as he got to where we were sitting.

'Excuse me?' I was taken aback.

He face suddenly split into a smile. 'Just kidding! You should have seen your face,' he laughed.

'Who is he?' Vatsala looked at me and asked. Loudly. She has no social skills. Absolutely zero, I tell you.

'Hey, I am Tushar Mehra.' He offered his hand and introduced himself.

'Hi. Vatsala Rathore. Chhavi's flatmate.' They shook hands.

'Nice to see you. Chhavi must have told you about me?'

There was a brief awkward moment before they both turned to look at me. 'I, er . . . he is the guy I told you about that day, remember? The *famous* photographer?' I stressed on *famous* to give the impression that I had been saying good things about him to her. Vatsala, however, decided to totally embarrass me instead.

'The guy you *think* you had unprotected sex with?' she asked innocently.

I met Tushar's eyes and we looked away. I nodded slightly at Vatsala and motioned to her to let the matter go.

'Oh, sorry. I should not have said it like that. That was awkward,' she said and bit her lip.

'I need a drink,' Tushar said. 'You girls want anything?'

We both shook our heads in *no*. He turned away to get his drink and we watched him go. We were like two crazed teenagers at a rock concert. There should be tickets costing shitloads of money just to get to see him. He looked *that* dashing. Vatsala whispered in my ears, 'He is so hot! Why didn't you tell me?' She was almost hyperventilating by then! Like me.

'Who is hot?' Ankit asked from behind, startling us.

'Oh, hi! Thank God you came. Chhavi is about to get *busy* with this guy. I would have died of boredom,' Vatsala said.

'What guy?' Ankit asked.

'That guy—there. In the black Batman T-shirt.' She pointed towards Tushar.

'Hmm . . . nice!' Ankit turned to me and winked. 'Hi. Why the sudden plan?'

'I hired an agent. So I figure I will be busier now. That is why I thought we would enjoy tonight.'

'Wow, that's great. A new agent—means more offers on the table, eh?'

'I certainly do hope so.' I smiled nervously.

'I'm sure it will be fine.' He smiled back. Just then, we saw Tushar make his way back towards us. 'Ankit Rai.' Ankit shook his hand as Tushar joined us back.

'Tushar Mehra.'

'He is Vatsala's boyfriend,' I supplied, as I looked at Tushar. We made small talk for a little while, before Vatsala pulled me away from the group.

'Can I talk to you for a minute? Alone?' Vatsala looked at me and said.

'Sure,' I replied. *No social skills*, I told you. Why did she just *have to* embarrass me? 'Excuse us, guys. We will be just a minute,' I added before I made my way to the women's room with Vatsala.

'You are leaving with him tonight?' Vatsala asked me as I reapplied my eyeliner in the washroom.

'I guess. I like him. Like—*a lot*,' I said.

'Great! So that means you don't mind if I leave with Ankit?'

'Of course. Why would I mind? He's your boyfriend!'

'I meant *now*. I want to leave with him *right now*.'

'Oh. Okay, whatever you wish,' I said.

'Thanks,' she smiled and her eyes lit up. I could see that she was excited. She had reasons. Her 'love' life was at its peak! While I was just making out with a random hot guy and waking up the next day without any memory. How romantic.

'May I ask why?' I asked, even though I already knew the answer. It is always fun to see Vatsala's expressions. She has *zillions* of them. I don't think she ever repeats one.

'I *need* Ankit. *Need. Now.*'

We laughed and went to join the guys at the bar. Almost immediately, Vatsala whispered something in Ankit's ears and within seconds, they excused themselves to leave.

'So?' Tushar looked at me, once we were alone. 'You wanna dance?'

'Not tonight,' I met his eyes and said. It had been quite a long time since I had been with a guy. And although I did not really mind, this guy did something to me. I could not wait to see what it would be like between the two of us. Somehow, even though I was sure that we would rock together, I could not really get a vivid picture of it in my mind. *Maybe I will have to do it with him first to imagine us together in bed.*

'So what *do* you want to do tonight?'

'Read my mind,' I said, getting straight into the act. I wanted to leave here with him. Fast.

He stared at me for a moment, pretending to read my mind, and said, 'Ew! That's so dirty! That's some really nasty stuff you want to do tonight.'

'Are you still interested?' I asked, naughtily. Somehow, with Ankit and Vatsala around me now-a-days, I too craved for something like what they shared. Or maybe, I was just being slutty.

'I think I will pass,' he shrugged.

'Okay then. I will look for someone else. Someone who knows how to kiss, at least.'

'Are you saying *I* don't know how to kiss?' he asked. He looked genuinely surprised. Aww. I hurt his ego. 'That kiss wasn't great?'

'Can that even be *called* a kiss? Eighth grade kids kiss like that!'

He stared at me for ten seconds straight. 'Really. Every time I start thinking that you're sweet, you say something to make me think otherwise.'

'That's me.' I smiled.

'Yes, I am beginning to know. And I would like to know more. Starting tonight.'

'Oh, yeah? But I thought you weren't interested anymore?'

'You made me change my mind . . .' he said sexily. It gave me chills.

'Really? Too bad, I kind of like that guy over there . . .' I said, motioning in the general direction of the dance floor.

He held me by the arm and guided me out of the disc.

~

'So? Will you call *that* a kiss?'

'Eh. You know—it was *okay*,' I said, even though I was still reeling from the impact of our kiss. Man! The guy knew how to kiss. What else could you expect from a guy with such amazing lips? And didn't I just love the way his stubble rubbed against my skin!

'Just *okay?*' He looked *very* offended. Guys and their big ego issues, I tell you.

'Yeah. It was fine,' I shrugged.

'I would like to meet the other guys who have kissed you.'

'Right. Maybe they could teach you a trick or two.' I nodded seriously.

He kissed me again, violently, almost to prove himself. If it was possible, that kiss was even better than the last. He broke away and cocked his head back to look at me. 'So?' he asked.

'I would give it a four.'

'On five?'

'On ten,' I said and looked at him. He couldn't be more exasperated.

At first, he looked at me as if I had totally lost my mind. And then he finally understood that I had been kidding. 'I guess I will just have to keep trying until I make it ten on ten, eh?' he said.

A shiver ran up my spine. He pushed me against the wall and pinned my body against it. His mouth came down on mine with extra force this time. His tongue battling with mine, as I surrendered myself to him. It wasn't anything like what I had thought a kiss could be. I had never experienced such passion in a kiss before.

He was still pinning me against the wall, as his hand crept down my arm to hold mine. I looked down to see his dark, tanned arm, against my pale skin. For some reason, it aroused me. His veins were prominent under his dark skin, and his palm felt rough against mine. It gave it a very masculine feel. I shivered in anticipation.

And then, he was kissing me again. And this time, it was not to prove himself. It did not have the rough, unveiled force in it.

This time, it had such subtlety that it felt as though the whole world had caved in around me, leaving me floating helplessly in a dimension I had never imagined existed.

The pressure of his mouth moving against mine was so elusive that I simply did not have any defence against it. I heard him make a sound deep in his throat, and felt a thrill in recognition of what it meant. *He wanted me.*

His hands were now caressing my throat, pushing aside the fabric of my dress. I could feel the fabric slide down my shoulder and seconds later, I could feel his lips against the skin he exposed there.

I made no attempt to do anything. I did nothing but clutch at his shoulders to steady myself. I was in some other world . . . but soon, I wanted more.

I held him by the collar of his tee and pulled him towards myself, looking into his eyes and smiling. I put my arms around his neck and he looked down at me, his hand creeping up on my thighs, under my dress.

That night was the best night of my life. We *destroyed* his hotel room. And we ran short of condoms. Yes, even though he had those four in his wallet. Now I knew why he carried so many of them with him! It seemed like I was a little too much to take, even for him.

Ha!

~

'Chhavi,' Tushar whispered in my ears.

I opened my eyes and looked at him. He was sitting completely dressed, on my side of the bed. It was morning after. *I had to go.* My head went back to last night. I remembered everything. *Brilliant.*

'I am sorry, but I have to check out of the hotel now,' he looked at me apologetically and said.

'Oh. Okay.' I sat up on the bed. *Oh God. This is so embarrassing. He is asking me to leave. To top that, I now have to pull away the sheet covering me, walk around the bed, naked and pick up my clothes lying across the room. The journey from the bed to the washroom is always the longest when the guy is awake. Plus—a guy should not see you naked for very long. It kills the charm for him. Been there, done that.*

'I will get your clothes,' he said and went to collect everything. I saw him pick up my clothes from around the room and I blushed pink. I had no idea how I could be so bold the night before, only to get back to my real self the next morning. This guy . . . he was really something. I knew it was all happening in the wrong sequence, but—I wanted to get to know him more. He was not someone a girl would just have a one night stand with and forget later on. And I was not a girl who ever had one night stands with guys.

'Thanks,' I said, eternally grateful, when he handed my clothes to me. If I had not feared looking like a slut, I swear I would have blown him.

'Sure,' he said and turned his back at me, letting me maintain some dignity as I made my way to the washroom. He pretended to fiddle with his already packed bags.

This guy is serious boyfriend material. I am never letting him go, I promised myself. Plus—I'll tell you a secret—he was *awesome* in bed too! I wondered if he did anything wrong ever.

I slowly made my way to the washroom, with my clothes. My reflection in the mirror was enough to scare me to death. I looked exceptionally hideous. Or maybe it was because the last person I saw was Tushar, and I stood nowhere in comparison. How can someone be so . . . *perfect?*

As I washed away my smeared eye makeup, I wondered if Tushar would ask me out. I was new to the whole concept of open relationships. I mean—yes, I had seen many around me, but I had never been in one. I had had very few relationships in my life, and I had been embarrassingly 'un-adventurous' in all of them. It had always been 'One guy, one girl, in love' sort of thing. I didn't know what to make of what I had with Tushar. 'One guy, one girl. Girl likes guy. Guy might like girl too. At least that's what the girl wants. No love . . . or was there? From which end? Was he serious? Was she? Plus—still unsure if there was actual love between the two—they did *make love* once. Or twice. Were they exclusive? Were they even seeing each other?'

You see? I was confused.

When I came out of the washroom, Tushar was ready with his backpack. 'I feel so bad about this,' he said at the reception, as he checked out.

'It's okay.'

'No, really. If I didn't have this flight to catch . . .'

'I understand. Don't worry about it,' I said. I was a little pissed off, but he looked so cute and worried that I forgave him.

'I'll make it up to you. Let me take you out sometime. I'll be here next week. Please don't say no.'

'It's really okay, Tushar. You don't have to—'

'I'm serious. Please. I feel so bad about this. Let me do this,' he said as we stood outside the hotel, and waited for our taxis.

'Is this your way of asking me out?'

'And making sure you say yes,' he agreed. 'Did it work?'

'It might have.'

'Is that a *yes*?'

I smiled.

He held the taxi door as I got in. As I saw him close the door and walk to his taxi, I felt exceptionally happy. I finally knew a nice guy after so long! Well, we made out twice in two dates, and that was not how you start something new . . . but, whatever.

I now had a vivid, *vivid* picture of us together in bed. It was awesome.

The Proposal

'How much longer?' Vatsala asked from where she was sitting on the counter-top in the kitchen.

'I have no idea. You tell me! You have the recipe!'

'Oh, right,' she said and checked the piece of paper she had been carrying around with her all morning. 'It says—steam for twenty minutes and . . .'

'Twenty minutes? But you had said forty before.' I immediately turned off the stove.

'Did I? Oh crap. My bad!'

'This is such a disaster,' I looked into the gooey material in the pan and said.

'Shit.'

We had been working all morning on a recipe Vatsala got from someone on the set. She swore it was the best dish she had ever tasted and she wanted me to cook it. I could not even pronounce its name. After asking her to repeat it four times, I gave up. It reminded me of the time when a friend of mine told me about some exotic sex trick. I still can't pronounce its name. And it should be forgotten anyway. It was gross.

She had been sitting on the countertop all morning, giving me instructions. Which, by the way, were *slightly* different than what they really should have been. So, we ended up screwing the whole thing up.

'Never mind. I will cook something else,' I said. 'But it will take time.'

'I cannot wait; I am starved. Do we have Maggi?'

'Yeah. It's in that cupboard behind—' I was interrupted by my phone ringing.

'Go ahead—receive the call. I will take care of this,' she said, and bent to take out the Maggi packets from the cupboard.

'Are you sure? You can cook?'

'Of course! Just because I *don't* cook does not mean I *can't* cook,' she laughed.

'But—'

'It is just Maggi. I can cook. I am not an invalid!' she said and looked rather offended.

'Okay,' I said and picked up my phone. *Ma calling*. 'Hello.'

'Chhavi, beta. How are you?'

'I am fine, Ma. How is everyone at home?'

'We are good. And we are all very excited . . .' she left it hanging.

'Excited about what? What happened?'

'Beta, there is a proposal for you . . .' she said. Not again! She wanted me to get married before I was successful. Or ended up in a condom ad. Then, I would be totally un-marriageable. 'Marriage proposal. The boy is Bengali too. And he—'

'But Ma, I told you—I'm not going to marry right now. I'm not ready yet,' I said for the millionth time.

'There is no such thing as *ready!* You just meet him and decide. We are not putting any pressure on you,' she said sweetly.

You cannot imagine how sweet and calm-tempered everyone at my home starts acting whenever they discuss my marriage. They know that forcing will not get them anywhere in this particular case.

'I told you I will let you know when I want to get married. Then why did you go looking for a groom?' I am very rarely angry, especially at my mom. And this was one of those rare times.

'We did not go *looking* for them. They came to us! You are pretty and you belong to a good family. And now you are of marriageable age. So it is obvious that proposals will come our way.'

Again. This was really getting old. They use this excuse every single time. I did not say anything.

'Beta, listen to me. He is a very nice guy. His family is very reputed. And he earns a lot,' she said.

'So? You are saying I should get married for money?'

'That is not what I meant. Not *only* money. But frankly, if we arrange a marriage for you, isn't it justified for us to look for someone who earns well?'

'Why are you arranging a marriage for me, in the first place?' I said and Vatsala stopped in her tracks to stare at me. She stared at my face for ten whole seconds, and then her eyes got all big and round in horror. She shook her head vigorously and mouthed *don't-get-married* again and again.

Ma sighed. 'You are not the only girl in the world getting married. We have our responsibilities to think of. We—'

'Ma, please. Enough with the emotional shit!' I suddenly burst out. I regretted it instantly. I shouldn't be rude; she was my mother, after all. But I don't know what happens to me whenever my marriage is being discussed. I turn into a mad, scary version of myself.

Mom's voice hardened. 'Alright. The guy, Sanjay, lives in Mumbai. Go see him if you wish to and don't if you don't. I have asked Priyesh to mail you this guy's bio-data and photograph.

Go through it if you have a few minutes to spare in your hectic modelling schedule—'

'Why do you just *have to* drag my career in every time? Where does modelling figure in all this?'

'It all starts there. You have done what you have wanted and we have always encouraged you to live your life and have fun. But you should start thinking about settling now.'

'But why? Why should I stop now? My career is going quite well—' I started to explain but she cut me off.

'I know how well your career is going. When was the last time you had a shoot?'

'Okay. Yes, I agree it has been some time now but things will get better. I have hired an agent. He is really good and he assured me that I will get—'

'Chhavi.' Ma sighed. 'You should know when to stop.' *What on earth does that mean?*

'I know when to stop. And it is definitely *not* now. Not yet,' I said slowly.

'Beta . . . you have been doing well till now. People know you. And we receive a lot of wedding proposals for you. But that will *not* last forever. Once your career starts deteriorating, people will not want to marry you.' *Or if you take up a condom ad.*

'You don't have to worry about that, Ma. I am sure I can find someone to marry me.'

'Is there a guy? Is this what this is all about? Are you in love with someone?'

'No, Ma. I am not going out with anyone at the moment,' I said, my mind suddenly drifting to Tushar. I was not lying. We had not gone on a date till then, so I had not started dating him officially. But that doesn't mean I did not want to. I wanted to. Gosh, I *so* wanted to.

Ma decided to bring me back to reality with her, 'Is there a . . . girl?'

'*What?* NO! Are you kidding me? Ma! What have you been watching? I am perfectly straight.' When you have to clarify to your mom that you are not a lesbian, you feel awkward. She was relieved.

'Oh. I just thought . . . with modelling and everything . . .'

'Listen Ma, I really have to go now. My breakfast is getting cold,' I said. 'I will go through the bio-data and the picture and let you know,' I added as an afterthought.

'Oh beta! That means you will consider?' I could hear excitement rising in her voice.

'Umm . . . I will see,' I said, not committing. 'You take care.'

'You too, beta.'

'Bye.' I hung up and made my way back to the kitchen.

'So, you are getting married?' Vatsala asked, as she served the Maggi.

'No way. I am definitely *not* getting married!'

'But you said on the phone that you would check out the bio-data and the photograph.'

'Yeah. And then I will tell Ma that I do not like him. I am not getting married yet,' I said.

'What if he earns shitloads of money? You still won't marry him?'

'Of course! How does that matter? Are you telling me that I should marry a guy just because he earns big money?'

'Yes, I am actually telling you to marry a guy who earns a lot of money. Why shouldn't you?' she replied casually, distracted with her Maggi.

'That would be so sluttish!'

'What? Marrying a guy for money does *not* make you a whore. Not marrying a guy for money makes you stupid.'

'Just exactly how? Would you please explain?' I asked.

'It's common sense. If you are having an arranged marriage, why would you marry a guy who does not earn good money?

It is like shopping. You are paying the exact same amount for the article, but *choosing* to buy the defective piece of the lot.'

'You are unbelievable! You are comparing marriage to *shopping*,' I said, stunned.

'Yes! Because it is the perfect example! Arranged marriage basically *is* like shopping. When you shop for shoes, you will see the brand, the style, the material, the colour, the comfort and how much it costs. Similarly, when you choose a guy to marry, you see the family background, the education, the looks, whether or not he likes Eminem, his sense of humour and the money. After all, your parents are the ones who would have to pay for the wedding arrangements. So why choose a lesser earning guy?'

'So if Ankit does not get all filthy rich in the future, you will not marry him?'

'What? No! Our case is different; *I love him*. I will marry him even if he sells peanuts! What I meant was—since you do not even know any of these guys personally, it makes sense to choose the best depending upon certain criteria. And money is definitely one of them,' she said.

'Hmm . . . you do have a point . . .' I brooded about it. 'Still . . . I don't know why, but just the idea of marriage gives me chills. I mean, what if he turns out to be some kind of a psychopath? Someone who is nice in front of everyone but is into some really disgusting sex stuff? What if he does . . . some kind of revolting acts in bed? And makes me do something equally disgusting? And hits me when I disagree to d—'

'Chhavi, stop please. You are scaring me.'

'Oh. I'm so sorry. I didn't mean to.' I sometimes forgot that Vatsala, for all her philosophies and insightful comments, was basically just a kid. Though she would never accept it!

'Never mind. Let's check the bio-data. I want to see what this guy is like,' she said and turned on her laptop.

'Oh please. Do we have to? I'll just call Ma and tell her I don't like him.'

'Come on. Just have a look. What if she asks you something about him?'

'You're right. She probably will ask me something,' I said.

'Password?' she asked and I gave her the password to my Gmail account. *No, I'm not telling you what it was.*

'There is an unread mail by Priyesh Mukharjee. Is that it?'

'Yeah, he's my brother,' I replied. I was sitting facing the back of the laptop and reading Vatsala's expression to gauge how bad the guy was.

'We will save the picture for later and check out his bio-data first. Looks don't matter. Sanjay Chatterji. Born 19 December 1985. So he is almost twenty-six. You are?'

'Twenty-one. He is five years older. No way.'

'It's not that bad! Five years can be considered. Six years would have been a *no way*,' she countered. And continued, 'Six feet. Fair, handsome, blah-blah-blah. Interested in painting, gardening, blah-blah-blah. Merit list in X and XII, college topper, blah-blah-blah. Works in an MNC here at Mumbai. Earns a package of thirty five lakhs per annum.'

'Thirty five? That's big. What does he do?'

'Works in the HR department.' I saw Vatsala scan the bio-data again. 'He seems perfect. I can't find any major flaw. Maybe you should meet him.'

'You think?' I asked, as Tushar's image suddenly flashed through my mind again. Three meetings with him, and he was all I could think about. I suddenly started to miss him. I wanted to see him again.

'Yeah. Call him and set a meeting. I will sit discreetly at a nearby table and note down my observations. Then we'll be able to evaluate better.'

'Are you serious?'

'Of course,' she said. And she looked very serious too.

'But I don't *want* to get married now.'

'You don't have to marry him right away. Meet him and see how things go. Ask him to wait and stuff,' she shrugged.

What about Tushar? I wanted to ask, but didn't. There wasn't anything accountable between the two of us yet. Though we definitely were pretty awesome in bed. And the picture, the vivid, *vivid* picture, hadn't left my mind yet. And it wouldn't, ever.

But I didn't know how Tushar felt about me. I might have been stupid enough to give my heart to him in a completely non-serious 'relationship' that I had with him, but what were the odds that he was equally into me? He was a photographer, who had a lot of models around him all the time. Maybe I was just one of those girls for him. Maybe I didn't mean anything. It would be foolish of me to expect otherwise.

I decided to stop brooding about it before I shoved myself into depression.

And this Sanjay character seemed way too perfect for me anyway. He was the kind of person who made others feel inferior. Remember that all-rounder kid from school? The one who was *so good* at *everything* he did, that you didn't even *think* of competing with him at anything. Exactly.

'Oh. My. God.' Vatsala's expression told me she had seen a ghost. She didn't say anything else, just shook her head. And kept shaking it.

I got up to see for myself and though I had never been and would never be as dramatic as Vatsala, I am sure that at that moment, my face displayed the exact same expression that hers wore.

The guy looked *out-of-the-world*. No, I don't mean the *good* out-of-the-world. I mean—no one on earth can ever look like that. He must have been an alien.

To start with, he was fat. Not a little bit *healthy*, but a solid twenty kilograms overweight. When a six-foot-tall guy was this fat he would look like a troll. And he did.

And he was fair. Actually, *fair* would be very misleading a term. He was *white*. White, like those vampires in the *Twilight* movies, remember? I would like to see him in the sun. I bet he would sparkle. And that is supremely gay.

No moustache. No beard. Which I obviously did not mind (though I had started to adore the rough stubble of a certain someone). The only thing bugging me was . . . for some reason, I thought he *didn't* sport them because he *couldn't*. He was one of those guys who didn't have to shave. Imagine.

He had a round face, with a big nose and really, *really* red lips. Not all Bengalis need to chew paan. And, you know, there was something about him that just screamed . . . well—*I'm impotent.*

Although all this must have been enough for you to picture what he looked like, I can't *not* tell you about his hairstyle. That would be so unfair to you. Because it was, by far, the thing I remember most clearly. And the thing we laughed the most at.

His hair was lubricated with a gallon of oil (mustard, is my guess), parted in the middle by an immaculately straight line and brushed to each side. The hair stuck to his head almost like a second skin. And the front hair fell on his forehead, hiding more than half of it, forming two semi-circles, one on each side.

Remember Salman Khan's hairstyle in *Tere Naam*? The front part of his hair looked *exactly* like that. Actually, even worse.

He kind of looked like a very warped version of Kishore Kumar from *Padosan*. The only difference was that Kishore Da actually looked pretty awesome in it, and this guy, Sanjay, looked like he tried copying it but failed miserably. Add to that those twenty extra kilograms. *Disaster.*

The only condition at which I would have agreed to marry him was if he sang as awesomely as Kishore Da. I would have been ready to overlook his every single flaw if he had that one quality. But I didn't remember anything relating to music in his bio-data. Hard luck.

Ma actually thought I should marry him? I *needed* to do something about my career. *Fast.*

After staring wordlessly at the picture for quite some time, I turned to look at Vatsala. She met my eye and we burst out laughing. We did the real rolling-on-the-floor-laughing that day. By the time we finally stopped, we had tears in our eyes and were clutching our tummies as it hurt from all that laughing.

'I don't think you should meet him. I don't think he listens to Eminem,' she said.

'He certainly doesn't look like someone who listens to Eminem,' I agreed. Vatsala is obsessed with Eminem. For her, he is like a God or something. But no matter how much she tried to force me to, I simply could not bring myself to like him. He is just not to my taste.

'But you can marry him, Chhavi. You won't have to worry about one thing . . .'

'What?'

'He's definitely not into any disgusting sex stuff. In fact, I'm pretty sure he can't even get it up.'

No Strings Attached

'If Ankit sent me this, he is having the time of his life tonight,' Vatsala said, staring wide-eyed at the huge bouquet of orchids sitting on the table. It was at least four feet tall and two feet wide. And it was beautiful. Obviously.

'What do you mean *if*? Who else would send you flowers?' I asked, not taking my eyes off the flowers for a second.

Vatsala stared at me wordlessly.

'What?' I asked.

'I'm not the only one living at this address, silly! They can be for you!'

'Me? Who will send *me* flowers? I have no idea,' I said, hoping against hope that they were from Tushar. Oh, I *so* wished it was Tushar! My heartbeat started to rise.

Vatsala read my mind, 'Tushar . . . maybe?'

'*Naah!* Ankit must have sent you those. Tushar and I don't share that kind of relationship,' I shrugged, trying not to get my hopes too high. I looked back at the bouquet. *Let it be from Tushar. Let it be from Tushar. Let it be from Tushar.*

'Ankit would have sent me roses,' she said matter-of-factly. 'Let's check?' she said, pointing to the small card hidden between the flowers.

'Okay,' I said. I was practically dying of suspense!

'There's no name, *for* or *from* . . .' Vatsala read out the note:

Let's face it—you like me.
See, there is no use denying.
You can't hide it anymore.
I know.

And . . . well . . .

Let's face it—I like you too.
Again, there's no use denying.
I can't hide it anymore.
You know.

So, I'll pick you up at six!
P.S. It was so clever of me to force you to accept!

We did not need a name.

'Tushar!' Vatsala let out. 'Too bad Ankit didn't think of doing something like this for me. I was feeling so generous today!'

I didn't say anything. I *couldn't* say anything. I didn't even hear what Vatsala said. I had a few things on my mind. *Tushar. Tushar. Tushar.* I smiled. Not smiled, actually. Blushed. *Terribly.*

I did not know I was still capable of being so foolishly in love. One minute—I was worrying if I even meant anything more than a fling to Tushar, and the next— I was blushing like a teenager who just got asked out for a dance by her secret crush. I actually had that stupid expression on my face. One would think that after all that *practicality* I had around me in my profession, I would have *grown up*. But no. I still very much believed in everlasting, eternal love. I was still very much the kid with a Tom Cruise obsession. Only, it had a different name now—Tushar.

'So, you're going out tonight?' Vatsala brought me back from my reverie.

I looked at the flowers, still smiling. She took that as a *yes*.

'And are you going to make out?'

I maintained a neutral expression. It was difficult. I was bursting with happiness inside.

'*What?* Tell me!'

'What do you think?' I said slowly.

'Tushar is having the time of his life tonight!'

I just smiled.

~

'He is here,' Vatsala called from the living room, letting him in.

'Just a second,' I called back. I hadn't asked him if and how he had my address. I knew he must have got it. Just like he got to know my name. And phone number.

'Do you need me?' Vatsala asked as she peeked into my room from the door.

Need Vatsala for . . .? Make up? Dress selection? Accessory matching? Deciding footwear? She didn't know the first thing about any of them. Although she did a pretty decent job putting together stuff from her own wardrobe, that didn't mean she could be any help with this. This wasn't denims and tees.

Still, not to sound rude, I asked, 'How do I look?' Okay I agree. I was a little nervous too. *Little*.

'Very pretty. Your hair's kind of twisted, though,' she observed.

'Twisted? Looks good or bad?' I had *twisted* it on purpose.

Had spent hours *twisting* it. And Vatsala can be the only girl in the world who would use the word *twisted* for it.

'It's okay, I guess,' she shrugged. And made a face.

In one swift movement, I removed the clip holding my hair and pinning it to my head and let the hair fall loose. I removed all the other pins as well. I looked at her questioningly, running my fingers through my hair.

'Better,' Vatsala nodded.

I turned to look at the mirror for the last time. I was wearing this gorgeous green dress from Guess that revealed quite some stuff, from everywhere. Still, it didn't make me uncomfortable in the least. Since I wasn't having any weight issues at the minute, it felt awesome to flaunt the figure I had worked so hard for. *And I knew Tushar would be watching.*

I grabbed my handbag and stepped into the living room. When I saw Tushar, I was glad he wasn't wearing some superhero graphic T-shirt. I am not saying I didn't like those, but they wouldn't have gone with my dress. I absolutely adored his shirt, though. It was charcoal grey and made him look like a dream. I could not take my eyes off him. I could not believe he was taking *me* out! It was too good to be true.

He looked at me—every inch of me—painfully slowly. When he was done, he looked into my eyes, wordlessly. They said it all, those eyes. Words were unnecessary.

'Shall we?' he gave me his arm.

'Sure,' I replied.

Vatsala kept shut, thankfully.

~

'So?' he asked, looking into my eyes suggestively.

'I don't know what you mean,' I said, knowing exactly what he meant.

'What do you want to do next?'

'What do you have in mind?' Even though I was not essentially a girl who flirted, whenever I was with Tushar, flirting came naturally to me.

'I had initially planned on taking you to Ra Lounge after dinner . . . but now . . . I don't think I'm particularly interested in drinking.'

'Why so? Any special reason?'

'I already feel drunk,' he said. 'I did not *need* to drink. You are intoxication enough.'

'So if not *Ra Lounge* . . . then? Where do you suggest we should go?'

'Back to my hotel.'

'You are *so* subtle, man! A complete gentleman,' I mocked.

'You want *gentleman*?'

'Umm . . . I think I prefer rogue.'

He smiled.

He took me to the Blue Frog that night and we had our dinner there. But since as a general rule, we made out more than we talked, it was getting kind of difficult for both of us to sit across the table, with no part of our bodies touching. It was kind of odd, I agree, to have spent more time with him naked, than with my clothes on, in all the time we had spent together since we first met. But it was kind of thrilling too. And I liked it.

Though I would not mind getting involved emotionally with him too. Because he seemed like a nice guy and he was definitely someone I would like to see on a more regular basis. Oh, who am I kidding? Didn't I already tell you that I was in love with him? I already felt a lot more than physical craving for him, but I was not sure what he felt, or what he was looking for. So for then—I decided—physical involvement would have to be enough.

And I was craving some physical involvement. I was doing a good job hiding how I was actually feeling at that minute. But Tushar wasn't even trying. He was quite visibly horny. *Quite.*

I thought about using my toes under the table, but didn't, owing to a sudden bout of pity for the poor soul. He had treated me very well that night. I had just one issue—he had not complimented me that night. Not even once. Not at anything. When you dress up for a guy—that too in a dress that costs you a sum of money that could feed a small village for a year—you definitely deserve a compliment. Correction—you *earn* a compliment. Still, after the flowers, and all the wining and dining, he did deserve to be spared the unnecessary misery. So I kept my toes in my pumps.

I bent a little forward on the table instead. A little exposed neckline would be enough to drive him nuts. And unlike toes, it would not be too cruel on my part either!

And I was feeling nice. Powerful. Had this been any other guy, I wouldn't have done anything of this sort in a million years. But this was Tushar, who somehow just had a way to wake the other, kinkier side of me.

'Chhavi . . . you know, you are the one who is going to have to pay for this later?'

'Pay for what?' I asked, with my super-innocent look on.

'You know exactly what,' he said. His eyes had that tortured look and he was gritting his teeth. He looked ready to take me then and there, on our table.

'Do I?'

'Oh, you *so* do.'

He had noticed what I had been trying to do. And it was working.

I shrugged as the waiter brought back his card. As we made our way to the car, Tushar put his hand around me, settling it on my waist. He leaned towards me and whispered into my ear, 'Just so you know, although you look exceptionally pretty tonight, the only thought that ruled my mind all night, looking at you, was—*such a waste*. So much time invested in getting all dressed up . . . when it's all coming off.'

It was a good thing he was holding me; I suddenly felt weak in the knees. I don't know how I made myself say, 'It wasn't a waste, after all. It served its purpose.'

'My point stays—it's all coming off. Soon,' he said and grinned wickedly.

His whispers, the occasional brush of his hands against mine, the passionate look in his eyes—they all sent me into tingles beyond imagination. It was as if we were already doing it.

The journey to his hotel room was hellishly long.

~

The first round was quick. Very quick. We didn't even make it to the bed. Or the bed room. Or even the hotel.

Car.

The second round was slower, longer. We explored each other's bodies leisurely, giving attention to the details. Even though the hot and heavy make out is almost always better, sometimes you just *need* the relaxed, lazy lovemaking.

And he was good at it. The way he took time to caress every inch of my body, left me writhing in pleasure. My heart beat off my chest and my breath got ragged. And I returned the favour, though the pleasure was all mine. His groans told me exactly what I was doing to him, and I relished the command I had over him.

As we lay spent, relaxing, preparing ourselves for round three, Tushar turned to his side to look at me. He had a strange expression on his face.

I raised my eyebrows questioningly.

'I want to say something . . .'

a sacrifice. I decided I'd just let it be physical for a while—like Tushar wanted—and see how it shaped up later on.

'Good for me,' he smiled.

'So . . .?'

'So . . .' he reached for me and pulled me closer, ready for round three.

'Let's use each other for sex.'

And we did.

'Sure. I am listening,' I turned to my side and paid attention. But he did not speak. He just kept staring at me.

'What is it, Tushar? You are scaring me now.' *Is he married?* No. I had Googled him. It had his full biography, but the mention of a marriage was non-existent.

'Chhavi . . . I really like you . . .'

'Okay . . .' I prodded him to say the rest. Even though he did not say it, the way he trailed off felt like a *but*. He likes me, but . . .? Girlfriend?

'And please don't get me wrong—but I like you more in bed.'

So the sex was great? I knew. We were awesome together. I had that vivid picture in my head too. And since the majority of the time we had spent with each other had been in bed, we barely knew each other as persons. So obviously, there was no competition between the two. Our make outs won hands down. I agreed. Then why was he so nervous about agreeing. What was the catch?

Or was that his way of saying he didn't like me? That it was just the make outs?

'See, I honestly do not have time for a full-fledged relationship,' he said.

Then I got it—he was brushing me off. *The sex was great, thank you. But you really aren't that great as a person. So, fuck off. With someone else.*

'Yeah, I know. Things are busy with me too . . . work-wise,' I said, as I tried to keep some dignity intact. I just had to make it as little insulting as possible. And although workwise my life wasn't that busy, I was sure it was going to be soon. I was sure Naitik was going to come up with something great for me pretty soon. So it wasn't exactly a lie either.

'Exactly what I mean. We are both young and we have our careers to take care of. In an industry like this, we have to stay alert and consistent if we don't want to become history.'

'Hmm. It is quite a struggle . . . being in this industry . . .' I replied vaguely.

'Right. And to top all that, I do not even live in the city. These weekly trips are not really enough to maintain a real relationship, are they?'

'Mmm . . .' I didn't know what to say. We were not even dating, and he was already dumping me. And somehow, being naked at the moment made me feel extremely vulnerable. I wanted to get my clothes on and run away as fast as possible. And I could feel the tears in the back of my eyes. They were coming, and it wouldn't take long for them to start to flow. I did not want Tushar to see me cry. *I wanted to run away.*

'But I really like you. I do not want to end this either,' he said in a low tone.

What? He was *not* blowing me away. He was just saying something and I was thinking something else. We were on two completely different pages right then.

'So . . . what do you mean, Tushar?' I asked.

'I just mean that I like you, but I have no idea how to deal with the whole situation . . . I don't know . . .'

'You're saying that you love making out with me. And that you like me. But you do not have time for a relationship? And you do not want this to end either?'

'Right,' he said.

'As I see it, there is only one way out.'

'What's that?'

'To continue this. Without the emotional attachments. Since we do not have time to reply to all mails and return all calls, we will simply . . . discard that face from our relationship. Keep it strictly physical. A simple, no fuss, no drama, only physical relationship,' I said.

'*Are you serious?*'

'Isn't this what you wanted?' I asked, wanting him to say *no*. This was one conversation I did not want to have. I knew how important his career was for him. And I knew I was too insignificant a part of his life to warrant him having to compromise on it. So, I knew this day would come. He would have to choose. And he would choose his career.

But I could not let him do that. *I could not let him go.* I knew that what we had had a very good chance to turn into something even better . . . something long term. And for that chance, I was willing to make do with a strictly-physical arrangement with him.

And that made me feel like a slut. But not quite. I hadn't been with him just for his body. I genuinely liked . . . maybe even loved the guy. And I really wanted to see what we could be in the future. It was too early to give up.

'Of course. But I did not expect you to agree,' he said.

'Why? We have been awesome in bed,' I said, and tried to act nonchalant.

'Yes, we have been. But that was with the thought of us getting together sometime in the future in the back of our minds. Now, with that aspect completely ruled out . . .'

'So now that I know there is no future with you emotionally, I should give up the physical part too?'

'I thought so,' he said, and studied my face. I tried my best to control my expressions. I hated the way he had said—*that aspect completely ruled out.* Was it? Did we really not have a chance at all? I was not willing to believe so.

'*Naah!* I know how to take things practically,' I lied easily. Well, okay. I will take the physical thing now and will see what can happen in the future. If we were meant to be with each other, things would work themselves out. With a *little* help from me. You do have to give up things for love, and this was too little

Love Follows

Strictly-intimate relationships are awesome. Why don't people do it more often? We had been doing it for a month now and it had been amazing. We had been meeting, usually late at nights, whenever he was in Mumbai and making out.

It was relaxing, he said. His career was so demanding that he just had to keep flying from one city to another all the time. In the month-long strictly-physical relationship that we had had, he had come to Mumbai six times. Four nights (which were legendary, of course) and two lunch breaks. The lunch breaks were pretty interesting too, with us running away to the nearest available hide-out and making out, in the middle of his shoot, when the rest of the set was eating their lunches.

Day-time called for hurried make outs and night time called for slow, lazy make outs. I loved both. And I found it relaxing too. How could I not? I mean—*it was Tushar!* And I am not referring to just how amazing he was in bed. I am also referring to how amazing he was otherwise too. He was such an adorable guy, with that twinkle in his eyes at all time and that stubble that he kept.

He made me laugh all the time and made all my stress go away. It was like we were already in an emotional relationship too, which we were, from my end, but I was still not sure about what he thought. It was hard for me to keep myself from falling even deeper in love with him. And I was not doing very well at it either. Anyway.

Although offers had not exactly started pouring in in ton-loads after Naitik took me up, he assured me that I was in a much better condition now. I could not see how, since I was still not in tremendous demand, but I had been doing things he had asked me to do and I was a lot more *visible* in the market now.

'So, did you go to the Kapoor's party last night?' Naitik asked that day. We were in his office, and he was dressed in this superb stark black suit that made him look even more lethal. I was a little scared.

'Yes, I did,' I replied. 'It was boring. The usual *loud-music-and-lots-of-liquor* stuff.'

'But at least the champagne was good, right? They are famous for it.'

'Yes! The champagne was the only thing that was good.'

'Never mind. You had some good champagne and that more or less makes up for the bad food. Anyway, it served its purpose.'

'It did?' I asked, excited now. In the past whole month, I had attended all kinds of events—product launches, parties, press meets and what-not on Naitik's insistence. He had believed that making appearances in all major dos around the city was the best way to make new contacts and refresh old ones. And he had always had passes ready for me.

'Sure. I am listening,' I turned to my side and paid attention. But he did not speak. He just kept staring at me.

'What is it, Tushar? You are scaring me now.' *Is he married? No.* I had Googled him. It had his full biography, but the mention of a marriage was non-existent.

'Chhavi . . . I really like you . . .'

'Okay . . .' I prodded him to say the rest. Even though he did not say it, the way he trailed off felt like a *but*. He likes me, but . . .? Girlfriend?

'And please don't get me wrong—but I like you more in bed.'

So the sex was great? I knew. We were awesome together. I had that vivid picture in my head too. And since the majority of the time we had spent with each other had been in bed, we barely knew each other as persons. So obviously, there was no competition between the two. Our make outs won hands down. I agreed. Then why was he so nervous about agreeing. What was the catch?

Or was that his way of saying he didn't like me? That it was just the make outs?

'See, I honestly do not have time for a full-fledged relationship,' he said.

Then I got it—he was brushing me off. *The sex was great, thank you. But you really aren't that great as a person. So, fuck off. With someone else.*

'Yeah, I know. Things are busy with me too . . . work-wise,' I said, as I tried to keep some dignity intact. I just had to make it as little insulting as possible. And although workwise my life wasn't that busy, I was sure it was going to be soon. I was sure Naitik was going to come up with something great for me pretty soon. So it wasn't exactly a lie either.

'Exactly what I mean. We are both young and we have our careers to take care of. In an industry like this, we have to stay alert and consistent if we don't want to become history.'

'Hmm. It is quite a struggle . . . being in this industry . . .' I replied vaguely.

'Right. And to top all that, I do not even live in the city. These weekly trips are not really enough to maintain a real relationship, are they?'

'Mmm . . .' I didn't know what to say. We were not even dating, and he was already dumping me. And somehow, being naked at the moment made me feel extremely vulnerable. I wanted to get my clothes on and run away as fast as possible. And I could feel the tears in the back of my eyes. They were coming, and it wouldn't take long for them to start to flow. I did not want Tushar to see me cry. *I wanted to run away.*

'But I really like you. I do not want to end this either,' he said in a low tone.

What? He was *not* blowing me away. He was just saying something and I was thinking something else. We were on two completely different pages right then.

'So . . . what do you mean, Tushar?' I asked.

'I just mean that I like you, but I have no idea how to deal with the whole situation . . . I don't know . . .'

'You're saying that you love making out with me. And that you like me. But you do not have time for a relationship? And you do not want this to end either?'

'Right,' he said.

'As I see it, there is only one way out.'

'What's that?'

'To continue this. Without the emotional attachments. Since we do not have time to reply to all mails and return all calls, we will simply . . . discard that face from our relationship. Keep it strictly physical. A simple, no fuss, no drama, only physical relationship,' I said.

'Are you serious?'

'Isn't this what you wanted?' I asked, wanting him to say *no*. This was one conversation I did not want to have. I knew how important his career was for him. And I knew I was too insignificant a part of his life to warrant him having to compromise on it. So, I knew this day would come. He would have to choose. And he would choose his career.

But I could not let him do that. *I could not let him go.* I knew that what we had had a very good chance to turn into something even better . . . something long term. And for that chance, I was willing to make do with a strictly-physical arrangement with him.

And that made me feel like a slut. But not quite. I hadn't been with him just for his body. I genuinely liked . . . maybe even loved the guy. And I really wanted to see what we could be in the future. It was too early to give up.

'Of course. But I did not expect you to agree,' he said.

'Why? We have been awesome in bed,' I said, and tried to act nonchalant.

'Yes, we have been. But that was with the thought of us getting together sometime in the future in the back of our minds. Now, with that aspect completely ruled out . . .'

'So now that I know there is no future with you emotionally, I should give up the physical part too?'

'I thought so,' he said, and studied my face. I tried my best to control my expressions. I hated the way he had said—*that aspect completely ruled out.* Was it? Did we really not have a chance at all? I was not willing to believe so.

'*Naah!* I know how to take things practically,' I lied easily. Well, okay. I will take the physical thing now and will see what can happen in the future. If we were meant to be with each other, things would work themselves out. With a *little* help from me. You do have to give up things for love, and this was too little a sacrifice. I decided I'd just let it be physical for a while—like Tushar wanted—and see how it shaped up later on.

'Good for me,' he smiled.

'So . . .?'

'So . . .' he reached for me and pulled me closer, ready for round three.

'Let's use each other for sex.'

And we did.

Love Follows

Strictly-intimate relationships are awesome. Why don't people do it more often? We had been doing it for a month now and it had been amazing. We had been meeting, usually late at nights, whenever he was in Mumbai and making out.

It was relaxing, he said. His career was so demanding that he just had to keep flying from one city to another all the time. In the month-long strictly-physical relationship that we had had, he had come to Mumbai six times. Four nights (which were legendary, of course) and two lunch breaks. The lunch breaks were pretty interesting too, with us running away to the nearest available hide-out and making out, in the middle of his shoot, when the rest of the set was eating their lunches.

Day-time called for hurried make outs and night time called for slow, lazy make outs. I loved both. And I found it relaxing too. How could I not? I mean—*it was Tushar!* And I am not referring to just how amazing he was in bed. I am also referring to how amazing he was otherwise too. He was such an adorable guy, with that twinkle in his eyes at all time and that stubble that he kept.

He made me laugh all the time and made all my stress go away. It was like we were already in an emotional relationship too, which we were, from my end, but I was still not sure about what he thought. It was hard for me to keep myself from falling even deeper in love with him. And I was not doing very well at it either. Anyway.

Although offers had not exactly started pouring in in ton-loads after Naitik took me up, he assured me that I was in a much better condition now. I could not see how, since I was still not in tremendous demand, but I had been doing things he had asked me to do and I was a lot more *visible* in the market now.

'So, did you go to the Kapoor's party last night?' Naitik asked that day. We were in his office, and he was dressed in this superb stark black suit that made him look even more lethal. I was a little scared.

'Yes, I did,' I replied. 'It was boring. The usual *loud-music-and-lots-of-liquor* stuff.'

'But at least the champagne was good, right? They are famous for it.'

'Yes! The champagne was the only thing that was good.'

'Never mind. You had some good champagne and that more or less makes up for the bad food. Anyway, it served its purpose.'

'It did?' I asked, excited now. In the past whole month, I had attended all kinds of events—product launches, parties, press meets and what-not on Naitik's insistence. He had believed that making appearances in all major dos around the city was the best way to make new contacts and refresh old ones. And he had always had passes ready for me.

'Yes. That fetched you another two offers. So, I have, let's see . . . seven offers for you right now,' he said.

'*Seven?*' I was shocked.

'Yes. But six of them are un-doable.'

'Why so?'

'Detergent, toothpaste, a role in a men's innerwear ad, sanitary napkins . . . I am not letting you do any of them,' he said with the usual finality in his voice. The *my-word-is-the-final-word* tone.

'But why? It is not like I am getting many offers anyway! Let's take this for now and the better offers will follow!'

'No! These are bad for your image. I am not letting you be seen covered in sweat, with a sad fucking expression on your face, washing filthy clothes on screen.'

'But toothpaste ads are better. I would just have to flirt with a guy—' I started to argue. But as always, his *no-arguments* tone cut me off.

'No, babes! That would imply you had bad breath, before you started to use that toothpaste. Now stop being such a smartass and let me do my work. You handle yours. Now, we will concentrate on better things.'

'Okay. Whatever you wish. Better things. Like?'

'Skin care products, hair care products, soft drinks, telecom network providers, apparels, footwear . . . you know, the kind of advertisements that people actually like?'

'Well, all ads are the same.'

'No, they are *not*. *I* tell you what is good and *I* tell you what is not. So just shut the fuck up.'

I nodded. I knew he was getting pissed. And I knew that for my own good, I should not piss him more.

'We will only take up ads in which you have to look good! We do not want you to be seen hassled and smutty. We want to see you shining and smiling. Right?'

'Right.' It was amazing that things like this came into his mind. I had never given such things a second thought in the two years I had spent in the industry. Maybe that is why he was the best in the business. My agent was a freaking genius.

'Good. So, we have footwear for you today. Still photo shoot. They need you for fitting today and the final—'

'Wait a minute—*today*?' I asked. Usually, such things are decided a little earlier.

'Yeah, I confirmed at the last minute. I was keeping the lines open for other offers. So, go to this place today at two o' clock,' he said, passing me a business card. 'They will not take much time. They will just take your size and stuff. The shoot is in three days.'

'Alright. Nice,' I smiled at him and turned to leave.

'And you have to go to that Jonas's stint tonight, remember?'

'Argh! I totally forgot. I can't go tonight. Tushar will be here. Please no . . .'

'Well, *Ms Madly in Love*, you just *have to* ditch your guy tonight and attend this. You do *not* have a choice,' Naitik declared in a dead-pan tone.

'But I can't! He is—'

'Actually, now that I think of it—you *do* have a choice . . . Since I am feeling all generous today . . . So, either you go to the party and I keep representing you. Or you do *not* go to the party and *fuck off* instead,' he shouted by the end of the sentence.

I said nothing. Shit. I was so looking forward to meet Tushar that night. It had been some time and I had been missing him. His visits to Mumbai were what I lived for.

'Totally your call. And in case you choose the latter, record it. Mail it to me. My porn collection is running really low. And I have always wondered what you hide beneath your clothes.'

I studied his expression to gauge how serious he was about this. He seemed very serious.

Oh crap.

~

'When can you come?' Tushar asked over phone that night.

'Not till eleven. This bloody shoot is taking forever to end. And then, there is this party I have got to attend . . .' I replied.

'Oh, hell.'

I smiled. 'It's okay. You get some sleep till then, you have had a hectic week.'

'But I don't feel like sleeping alone. I want my bolster. I want you.'

I smiled again. 'And you will have me. Soon.'

'Four hours is not *soon*. I want you *right now*!'

'Aww, come on! I am stuck here. I have no way out.'

'Shall I come? To your shoot? I want to see you, so badly,' he said.

'Umm . . .' I thought about it for a minute. *How difficult will it be to get back into my costume after we make out? Where can I find a secret place where we can make out? Will I be able to disappear from the set without being noticed?* The answers weren't very satisfying. And also, I didn't feel that Tushar wanted me only for my body. He said he wanted his bolster. It clearly meant that he wanted me close for reasons other than sex. I almost dared to hope that he was falling for me too. 'I don't think so. See, I don't have a problem with you coming, Tushar. I just cannot guarantee that we will be able to run away and make out even if you do come.'

'I know that. But . . . what if I still want to come? Just to see you. It has been over a week . . . I have missed you,' he said, making my heart skip a beat.

'That's so sweet,' I said, smiling ear to ear. He missed me too! *He missed me too!* 'But I still don't think you should come. It is an hour long drive, and you are already exhausted from all the work you had been doing recently. You need to rest.'

'I'm okay. I can take it. I'm coming. I cannot wait anymore to see you.'

'I will come straight to you when I am done here, Tushar. Don't come.'

'But I—'

'Sleep. I'll come wake you up.'

~

I did not need to wake him up. When I got to his hotel, he was already up. 'Hey,' he said, and moved away to let me in.

'Hi. You didn't sleep?'

'I did. Right after the call. Woke up just half an hour ago. Have you had your dinner yet?'

'No. I came here straight. You haven't eaten either?'

'No. I was waiting for you.'

'Really?' I asked, surprised. And touched.

'No! I was sleeping, remember? Had just woken up and taken a shower when you came . . . and I wanted to eat with you.'

I smiled.

We called room service and shared a dinner. It felt nice. This relationship—however shallow it might seem to a third person—was very fulfilling. It had all the perks of a real girlfriend–boyfriend relationship, only with infinitely hotter sex. Minus all the nagging and the fuss.

Plus the added bonus—we actually liked each other's company. So it wasn't like we were eager for the other person to run away as soon as we are done with the sex. On the contrary, the *before* and *after* moments were fun too. He was a really interesting person and I loved talking to him. He was one of those people with whom you feel like you can actually converse. I told him about things happening in my life—the career, the agent, the family's pressure for marriage. He listened. And he gave his perspective on the matters. It was refreshing.

And although he told me things about his shoots and everything, he never went into much detail. I didn't either. We never had that much time. Whenever we were together, we were always too busy unbuttoning or unzipping. And when we were not together, there were no phone calls, no text messages, no emails, no keeping in touch through social networks. One of the hazards of such a relationship—I never got to talk to him, unless I actually met him. I don't know how he dealt with it. I—for one—had a lot of difficulty doing the same.

Or maybe it was because I was the only one in love.

I waited for him in the bed as he tipped the waiter who was clearing the plates. When he left, Tushar came towards me. That always gave me chills—watching him walk towards me, knowing what would follow. The anticipation.

I pulled him towards me by the neckline of his tee and he pushed me down on the bed. Then he climbed over me and held my head in position. 'Did I tell you, you look gorgeous today?'

I blushed and said nothing.

'And that I love it when you blush?'

I blushed again, still saying nothing.

He looked into my eyes and smiled before bending and kissing my nose. 'You're so sweet,' he said.

And then he kissed me. One kiss was all it took to transfer me to some other world. He had that kind of power over me. By the time we broke the kiss, I had started to hyperventilate. I moved back a little and looked into his eyes. He held my gaze as I helped him out of his T-shirt and ran my fingers on his back, pulling him closer. He held the laces holding my spaghetti and pulled. And then he devoured me.

Every touch, every kiss, every bite . . . everything he did to me sent me straight to heaven. No one had made me feel the way Tushar did. His fingers weaved magic around me, his touch left me craving for more.

We had been making out for quite some time by then, but every time I thought it could not get any better, he surprised me. Every time was better than the last time.

Or maybe it was because of us, and our feelings towards each other. As time passed, our bond got stronger. Even though we had that unspoken agreement not to fall in love—which I had already, secretly broken—I thought we had come too far for the not-falling-for-each-other business. I thought he had fallen a little for me too. Or maybe it was just wishful thinking.

Half an hour later, as he lay asleep next to me, with one of his hands lying casually—yet strangely possessively—on my waist, I stared at the ceiling, wide awake. One thought ruled my mind—*he was in love with me. Oh, he was so very much in love with me.*

The only thing stopping him from acknowledging so was that he knew that we could not date. And the strictly-physical arrangement we had gave him a license to run away from his feelings for as long as he wanted. He had me with him whenever he was in the city, and that seemed to be enough for him for then.

Not that I minded. Our arrangement was running fine for me and I was having a real good time. And since I was not very sure about the intensity of my own feelings for him, I was in no rush . . . as long as it did happen sometime in the future. I could feel the love he had for me, and I was willing to wait for him to acknowledge the same.

No one knows what the future holds. Maybe we'll get together. Maybe we won't. It doesn't matter right now. Not yet. We'll worry about it when the time comes.

I turned to my side and looked at him sleep. I moved forward to kiss him lightly on the cheek. Coming back down, I rested my head on his chest, closed my eyes and smiled.

Hell. Who was I fooling? Did I say I was not sure about the intensity of my feelings for him? Well, I was just running away from the reality too. The intensity of my feelings for him was *inhuman*. My obsession for him was *Twilight*-level.

I was definitely very much in love with him.

The Wedding Reception

'I'll have to sell myself to buy that dress,' I said sadly, as I looked at a picture of the bronze Fendi piece I had seen in the buyers' catalogue that day.

'And why do you need that dress?' Vatsala asked.

'It is Tara's wedding this weekend and I have to attend it. She invited me. And Naitik asked me to attend as many dos as possible.'

'Yeah, but why do you need a new dress for that? Wear something from your wardrobe. You have so many dresses already.'

'You don't get it! This is *very* important. *Everyone* is coming. Why do you think Allya bought a new dress?' I tried to make her understand.

'So, you want to get a new dress just because Allya got one? Third graders do stuff like that.'

'I am not buying it just because Allya got one! That is not how this happened. It is just that when I saw that dress . . . you know how we fall *completely* in love? In the purest form? Unconditional. Irrevocable. Selfless. Absolute.'

Vatsala nodded vigorously in agreement. 'Just like I love Hershey's. *Every* chocolate it makes, I totally adore. Kisses, milk chocolate, dark chocolate, Mr Goodbar, Krackel—'

'Exactly,' I cut her off. You should never let Vatsala start on the topic of chocolates. She would never stop, trust me. So, I continued before she could say more, 'So you see? That is how bad I want that dress.'

'Oh. Now I get it. So buy it. How much is it for?'

'USD 649.'

'That is about thirty grands. Which is like an insane lot! Why waste so much money on a dress? I can have my Hershey's stock loaded for two years straight with that kind of money.'

I stared at her in disbelief. It was useless reasoning with Vatsala. First—she compared Fendi to Hershey's, which is as outrageous as comparing Fendi to . . . well, Hershey's! Then—she said I would be *wasting* my money on the dress. Waste? Buying good dresses is always an *investment*. Didn't she know? Wasn't she a girl? And then, she more or less said that her two years' expense of chocolates was about thirty grands. Actually, that was only Hershey's. She was a big Kirkland fan too, I had noticed.

She was mad.

So I gave up trying to make her understand and tried to think of a way to get that dress instead. Damn Allya. She shouldn't have forced me to sit with her and help her choose a dress online in the first place.

It was her fault that I was in love. With something that I would never have. Because I simply did *not* have that kind of money to spare. And I would *not* take out money from my savings for this. No, not even for Fendi.

Oh, chuck it. I am never getting that dress, I thought. I might as well just RSVP Tara that I won't be coming to her wedding.

About five seconds after I had mailed her, my phone buzzed.

'Chhavi! Are you freaking out of your mind? How the hell can you cancel at the last minute?' Tara shouted over phone.

'I am so sorry, Tara. I really—'

'I will listen to no excuses at all. I have the seating arrangements planned and you decide to bail at this time? This is simply unacceptable.'

'But I—' I started but she did not let me speak.

'I really do not have time for this. See, you said you will come and I put you in the arrangements. So you *have to* come. And bring a date.'

'Date? How am I supposed to find a date so quickly?'

'Yes, a date! Didn't you already say you were bringing a date?' she asked.

'I don't—'

'See, just grab a guy and force him to spend a couple of hours with you. That shouldn't be all that difficult. Flaunt your cleavage a bit. Or maybe even flash him one of your boobs.'

'Tara, I do *not* do stuff like that. I cannot do that to get a guy to come with me,' I said as sternly as I could muster.

'I don't freaking care! Strip for him. Blow him for all I know. But bring a guy with you,' she said and hung up.

~

'You know, you owe me one. And you owe me big,' Ankit whispered in my ear.

'I know,' I replied, as I looked at Allya. She was dressed in a small piece of cloth she chose to call a *dress*, dancing—grinding, literally—with a dark, tall guy she had met at the wedding reception.

'Good,' he said, looking away from Allya and wearing an expression on his face that screamed *what-the-hell-am-I-doing-here*?

I will tell you what the hell he was doing there—he was being Allya's date for the night. When Tara had forced me to bring a guy, I had asked Ankit to be my date and he had agreed. But then Allya had called, asking for help to find her someone.

And I knew that as desperate as she was, she might actually go for the options Tara had put forward for me over phone that day. Allya would actually have stripped or given head to a guy to get him to be her date that night. And I could not have let that happen.

And so, I had turned to Tushar for help. See, I was not essentially the jealous type, but with a guy like Tushar, you just *had to* be careful. He was some serious hot commodity in the dating scene. And Allya was pretty. Actually, she was so beautiful that *pretty* seemed like too insignificant a word. So I had not wanted to take any chances.

So, in the end, I had come with Tushar and Ankit had to be Allya's date. And now, Allya had decided to totally embarrass us in front of everyone. She had started drinking as soon as we got to the wedding, and by the time the reception started, she was heavily drunk.

So while she was busy creating a mess on the dance floor, we stood at a corner of the hall, and tried to pretend we didn't know her.

'The party is kind of nice, though. Some consolation, man,' Tushar said.

'I would have preferred staying out of the party, playing the valet, if given a choice. Trust me,' Ankit replied.

'Sure! Parking cars would have been better than being called Allya's *boyfriend*,' Tushar laughed.

Ankit glared at me.

'What did I do? *She* told everyone that you guys were seeing each other. I did not,' I said in my defence.

'And you are the one who asked me to be her date.'

'How was I to know that she would get drunk and create such a scene?'

'I know. It is not your fault. Still . . .' he trailed away and we all turned to look at Allya. The dark, tall guy she was grinding into seemed to have ditched her and was now making out with a younger model on a couch, right in the middle of the club. Allya was still on the dance floor, swaying to the music, looking around, as if searching for someone else to dance with. She looked as if she would pass out any moment; her knees buckled up a little every now and then. She needed help.

We turned to Ankit. He saw us looking at him and turned to look at Allya. A frightened expression came on his face almost immediately. Still, the gentleman that he was, he took a step forward to go to her.

'Let me handle this,' Tushar kept a hand on Ankit's shoulder to stop him.

'Thanks, man,' Ankit said and looked eternally grateful.

We watched Tushar as he made his way to the floor, dodging drunk people, who were falling all over each other. He looked extremely sexy that night. I would never forget that navy blue blazer he wore. I had never seen him in anything except T-shirts, other than that shirt he wore to the Blue Frog on our first official date. So this was different. And this was sexier. I could not wait to . . .

'You love him, don't you?' Ankit broke my train of thought.

'Umm . . . well, I *think* I do . . .' I replied, trying to hide my true feelings.

'And what about him? He loves you too?'

'I am not very sure. What do *you* think?' I tore my eyes off Tushar to look at Ankit.

'I think he does,' he smiled.

'I think so too,' I smiled back and we turned to look at Tushar. He reached Allya and tried to say something in her ear.

She turned to him and put her arms around his neck, pulling him close. I saw her mouth move as she said something to him and he threw his head back in laughter. I pursed my lips, dodging Ankit's eye. I knew he was looking at me. And I knew I had gone a little pink in the face.

As I saw them together, I could not help feeling supremely jealous of the way Allya's body was touching Tushar's. The way she was clinging to him made me feel like someone had stuck a hot iron rod in my throat. I felt the constriction.

Tushar put his arm around Allya's waist and made her move. As they came towards us, I saw her snuggle closer to him, literally falling all over him. They had just joined us at the table when I saw Tara coming to us with her brand new husband. Nice time she had chosen to make her social rounds around the reception.

'Congratulations,' I smiled, getting up to hug her. 'You were wonderful tonight. Your dress is beautiful.'

'Thanks a lot. I am so glad you could make it,' she said, looking so blissfully content, I automatically forgot all about what had transpired a minute ago. And thankfully, Tara was far from the scarier version of herself that she had been on phone one day ago.

'You guys look great together,' I said to Tara.

'So do you,' she said, looking behind me at the table. She was referring to Ankit, as Tushar was still partly in Allya's embrace. *Envy. Pure and unadulterated.*

I wanted to introduce Tara to Tushar, but he was busy keeping Allya from falling. I held back a lot of emotions brewing inside me, and turned to introduce Ankit instead. 'Tara, this is Ankit Rai. He is with me. And Ankit, this is Tara and her husband, Jason.'

'Nice to meet you,' Tara said as she held out her cheek for Ankit to kiss.

'Pleasure,' Ankit smiled politely and went ahead to shake Jason's hand.

'Hey Tara! Look who I have got here—Tushar Mehra!' Allya suddenly started to shriek. 'And guess what. He is my boyfriend!'

'Really?' Tara smiled and asked.

'*Really!* And we are getting *married* and we are gonna live together in the *mountains*. Aren't we, Tushar?'

'Of course,' Tushar looked down to see her face and said.

'And we are gonna have babies. *Five* babies!'

'Five? Isn't that a bit too much?' Tushar laughed.

'No! I want *five* of them! I want five!'

'Okay, okay! Whatever you say, baby.' Tushar turned to Tara and said, 'Excuse us please, she has had a little too much to drink tonight.'

'Oh, it is okay. We understand,' Tara replied. 'Thank you so much for coming, all of you. Now if you'll excuse us . . .' Tara said and left with Jason to attend another table.

'Let's go?' I looked at Tushar and asked.

'Sure. Ankit, would you—?' Tushar started to say.

'Let's make a baby! *Tonight!* Tushar, take me home, let's make a baby!' Allya started to shout again.

'Relax, we have all the time in the world. We can—'

'*NO! Tonight! I wanna do it tonight! NOW!*'

'Allya—'

She cut him off for the third time. *Only—this time with her mouth.* She was suddenly clinging on to him and pulling his face down by the hair. The way she fit her body between his made me want to die. She pressed her body to his, chest to chest, face to face, kissing him all tongues. I stood there, dumbstruck, as I watched them kiss. The scene was too much for me to take. My heart felt like someone had stepped over it. Ruthlessly.

But what hurt me the most was Tushar's reaction. At first, he looked shocked. But soon, as he realized what was happening, he started coaxing her away from himself, slowly loosening her hold on him and pushing her back. I don't know what I had expected him to do instead, but this certainly was not it.

Maybe he could have forced away the bitch off himself roughly? That would have felt better to me.

When he was finally out of her hold, he turned to look at me. I must have looked terrible.

'We should get her home,' Tushar said softly.

We stayed silent, no one said anything. No one knew what to say. Since they had come together, as an unspoken rule, Ankit and Allya were supposed to go back together. But I could not ask that of Ankit. If she did something of this sort with Ankit too . . . no, I could not do that to Vatsala. Knowing the risk, I could not ask Ankit to take Allya home.

But that meant Tushar had to take her home instead. Which also meant . . . I didn't even want to think what it meant. If *this* can happen in front of three hundred odd people, we don't need to be geniuses to tell what could happen when they're alone. I didn't want to suggest anything, so I maintained silence.

'I will get her home,' Ankit said.

Thank God!

'Thanks, man . . .' Tushar said and extracted Allya from himself.

Ankit held her by her elbow and guided her out of the club. 'Will you make babies with me?' I heard Allya ask as they left.

We had barely had time to even look at each other after they left when we were interrupted.

'Tushar Mehra!' a voice boomed across the hall and we turned to see Mr Valli come towards us.

'Go. Wait for me outside. I will be just a minute,' Tushar whispered in my ear and I left promptly. After all that had transpired that day, I was in no condition to face Valli again.

In fact, I was not in a condition to face *anyone* at the time. *Especially Tushar.*

As I stood outside the club and waited for him, I suddenly felt too tired to wait anymore. No, I was not angry at him. Although him calling Allya *baby* was unnecessary, the whole thing was not his fault. So, obviously, I did not hold anything against him.

But what bothered me was that if I went back with him, in the condition I was in, my expression would give everything away. He would sense something wrong and he would ask questions. We would discuss things. And in the process, it would come out loud and clear that I loved him. He was sure to realize exactly how madly I was in love with him. And since he did not know yet that he loved me too, it would seem pathetic.

I was not in a condition to deal with all that. Not yet.

I ran.

The Closed Chapter

'Hey, are you okay?' I asked, as Vatsala got into the apartment. I had been sitting in the living room, brooding about Tushar ever since I had come back from my shoot. I missed him and I missed him very, very badly. But I just could not bring myself to face him or even talk to him yet. I did not know what I would say to him, without making it glaringly obvious that I was head over heels in love with him. I was not very good at masking my expressions or tone. I would not be able to pretend . . . and he would get to know.

He had already made it clear that he could not get into a full-fledged relationship with me. And I had agreed. So if he got to know that I had fallen for him, he might just run away from me forever. After all, we had an arrangement, and I was the one breaching it. I did not want to lose him. Just the thought of it kept me up for nights in a row.

God! I could not afford to lose him . . .

I was not doing very well myself. But the look on Vatsala's face was something even I could not miss. Something was definitely up. And I just had to know what.

'Yeah, I am fine . . . Is it that obvious?' she asked.

'Something is up. Yes, it is written all over your face. Tell me—what is it? Something happened with Ankit?'

'No, no. Stuff with Ankit is cool.' She thought for a minute before saying, 'I met Ronit.'

'Ronit? You mean . . . *your* Ronit? Ronit Oberoi?'

'Yes. *My* Ronit.'

'Oh my God. How did this happen? When? Where?' I asked.

'After the shoot today. He was there at the set. He had come to meet someone.'

'And you met him? As in, actually talked to him and stuff?'

She nodded and I sighed with relief. Now that she had finally met him, she must have realized that he was just another regular guy. That he walks and talks like the rest of us. That he was not exactly God. And so, she must be over him. *Finally.*

'And . . .?' I asked. I wanted to hear the rest of it.

'And I . . . well, I liked him. He was nice,' she said carefully, as if measuring her words.

'And did he . . . did he know who you were?'

'Yeah. After I introduced myself, that is. He remembered my name from Facebook. And we talked. For about five minutes . . .'

'About what?' I asked. She was clearly hiding something.

'Nothing in particular . . . just generally. Small talk,' she shrugged.

I stayed silent for a minute, waiting for her to say more. Her expression said there was a lot more to the story. But she chose to keep silent too.

'Vatsala. Look at me,' I prodded and she met my eye. 'Now, speak.'

'I, er . . . Chhavi, I liked him. I *liked* him. He was so awesome. He turned out to be everything I had thought him to be . . . and more.'

'Oh God,' was all I could say.

This was bad. This was very bad. In all the time I had spent with Vatsala, the only time she had sounded this distraught was when she had spotted a lizard in the restroom. She had made me get rid of it, before getting back to normal. Other than that, I had always seen her take everything in the world lightly. But as she told me how awesome Ronit was, she looked extremely scared.

And I do not blame her for being so. Who wouldn't be? *Crushes are bad*, I tell you. You might think, after a week, a month or a year that it has blown away, but you are just fooling yourselves. Crushes never die. They are there. They are always right there . . . just waiting for a stimulus.

And instances like this play a major role in rekindling them. The moment when you realize that the guy you once had the hots for is still that awesome. That you still like him. And then, you need to do whatever you can to prevent it from blowing out of proportion.

Especially when you are committed to someone else. Which was the case with Vatsala. I could well imagine her plight.

'What do I do now, Chhavi?' Vatsala asked in a low voice.

'Damage control. Stop thinking about him. It is not like it will help anything. You will just fall harder for him . . .'

'I don't want to. I want to think about him all the time . . . And it is not like it would help even if I try forgetting. It has happened before. Nothing helps in Ronit's case. I just keep falling harder for him.'

'I know. But you *cannot* let this happen, Vatsala. This is unacceptable. Call Ankit,' I said.

'And should I . . .?'

'Tell him about Ronit? No. Not yet. You are not thinking straight right now. If you tell him now, he would probably gauge how you feel. And he would be hurt. Just call him and talk to him generally now. Later, when you are over this episode with Ronit, you can tell him all about it.'

She nodded thoughtfully. Just then, her phone started to ring and she looked at the display, and smiled. 'Hey, Ankit.'

I had to make that call. I just could not put it off any longer. Ever since I had left—ran, actually—from the club after Tara's reception, Tushar had been calling me. His calls were slowly getting less consistent, and it was beginning to worry me. If I continued ignoring his calls for much longer, he might just forget that a certain Chhavi even existed.

And I was missing him. Terribly.

He had been in Mumbai for the past whole week and I had met him just once—at the night of the reception. I knew he was leaving that day. And I did not know when he was coming back. *Oh man. What have I done?* When we got to meet just once in a week, we waited all week for that day to come. And now that he had spent the whole week there, I met him just once. And that one occasion was such a waste too. We did not even get to talk properly. All the time we had together was wasted at Tara's reception, in the midst of hundreds of other people. And . . . Allya.

So, it had been two weeks since we had made love and one week since we had talked. Obviously, I was missing him like crazy. And I knew he must be really mad at me.

I knew I was being stupid, continuing to be in misery and *probably* (translation—*hopefully*) making him go through the same, but I did not see any other way out. I was scared of facing him. I did not want to come across as a stupid starry-eyed teenager madly in love with a man who was interested in nothing more than her body and sometimes having a meal with her. Maybe even that was because he preferred my company to eating alone. Any company is better than no company.

Crap. I was overthinking again. It's amazing how I have always had the ability to shove myself into depression. I start with a thought and ultimately take it somewhere off the mark, reaching an extent of paranoia. That's one thing I still need to work at. Anyway. Given all the signs—I had a pretty good feeling that he had real feelings for me too. Just that . . . I was afraid. It was all too good to be true.

Finally, after brooding for a few more hours, I picked up my phone and my courage and made the call.

'Yes?' he said in a mechanical tone.

'Tushar . . .' I said meekly.

'Yes?' Okay, so this was just plain unnecessary. He had called me about a dozen times in the past week, and now he was acting as if he did not even recognize my number. And my voice. It hurt.

'This is Chhavi,' I said softly.

'Yeah, say,' he said, his tone not changing in the slightest.

'Can we talk?'

'Sure. What's up?'

'Tushar, please don't act like this . . .' I pleaded.

'Sorry?'

'You know what I mean.'

'I don't. And I don't have time to play any games either,' he said harshly.

'Hey, please at least listen to me. I'm really—'

'Listen, I have to go now. I have work to do. I will call you . . . sometime.'

I didn't say anything. He was acting so aloof, so detached . . . almost as if he didn't even know me. As if we were just acquaintances, just someone he met at some party once. His tone killed me. This was like my biggest nightmare coming true—that I did not mean anything to him. That all I had with him was just a passing . . . fling. Tears filled my eyes.

'Please Tushar . . .'

'What?'

'Talk to me . . .'

'I told you—I have work to do. What part of it don't you understand?' he suddenly shouted.

I didn't know how to react. I had expected him to be angry at me and I knew it was justified. But I had not been ready to face the anger. I had never seen him angry. I didn't know he would shout at me like that. He was acting like a complete stranger. I kept silent, as a few teardrops trickled down my cheek.

He kept silent for a while too, before I heard him sigh and say in a low voice, 'Chhavi? Baby, I will call you back. I promise. As soon as possible, okay?'

'Hmm . . .' I said.

'Now, please stop crying. Cheer up. Smile for me.'

'But . . . you are mad at me.'

'Yes, I am. I am very mad at you. And you are going to have to pay for it,' he said wickedly.

'Tushar—'

'Hush. I have thought of ways by which I will make you pay. When I call next, I will put forward options. I will give you a chance to pick the least painful one. The options have one thing in common, though—they all require you getting rid of your clothes.'

'Tushar . . . Please be serious.'

'Okay,' he said softly. And I noticed the sudden change in his tone.

'I'm sorry . . . I really am. I don't know what got into me . . . I tried, but I just could not face you after that . . . What happened with Allya that night . . . it was hard for me to see. I don't know why . . .' I said, trying to hide the fact that I was so obviously in love with him.

'Hmm . . .'

'I shouldn't have ignored you like this this whole week . . .'

'And you shouldn't have run away like that that night,' he added. 'Do you have any idea how worried I was about you?'

'That's nice to know,' I smiled. After all the insecurities I had felt all week, it felt nice to know that he cared.

'Chhavi . . . please never do that to me again . . .'

'I won't. Promise. I'm sorry . . .'

'Umm . . . You will be forgiven, for sure . . . once you pay for it.'

'I can't wait!'

~

And I didn't have to wait for long. He made me pay for the hell I had made him go through the whole week. And I paid happily. In fact, all his options were so interesting, that I didn't even need to select one. *I did it all.*

Okay. Who am I kidding? Truth be told—he did *not* make me pay for anything. I had missed him too much to waste time in such silly games when we were finally together. And apparently, he had missed me too. So—amazingly—none of the things we did that night involved me getting rid of my clothes.

We just talked. He held me while we were at it, and it felt nice to be in his arms. I felt like freezing the moment right there. It was perfect. The woody smell of his cologne, the slightly rough texture of his stubble on my shoulder—where he rested his chin, while he held me from behind as we sat talking—the baritone of his voice as he whispered into my ear, the soft, yet possessive, hold of his arms around my waist . . . it was just perfect. I could not have asked for a better setting.

I wondered when he would finally realize that he loved me too. His ignorance was reaching a level of sheer dumbness by that point of time. How could he *not* know?

He said, 'You know, you really didn't have to waste the whole week like this . . . We could have spent some time together. It would have been fun.'

'I know . . . but I just . . . I couldn't get that image out of my head,' I said honestly.

'And you were jealous?'

'I shouldn't be?'

'We're in an open relationship . . .' he said.

'Hmm . . .' I didn't say what was on my mind then. *Yes, we are in an open relationship. So? I'm not allowed to fall in love with you? I'm not allowed to want to kick a girl when she touches you? I'm not allowed to die a little when I see a girl snog you like that right in front of me?*

'Chhavi?' Tushar's voice broke into my thoughts.

'Yeah?'

'I liked that you were jealous.'

That's because you love me, moron. I smiled.

Soon, he dozed off and I sat up on the bed to look at him properly. We were not meeting for a fortnight, imagine. How would I be able to handle the distance? *How was I supposed to breathe?*

Just getting to look at him properly, so up close, was amazing. The dull light the night lamps emitted fell over his face, outlining it. I wanted to run my fingers over his face, but I was afraid that it would wake him up. And then it would be awkward. I had never really got a chance to actually stare at him properly. It might sound corny, but I wanted to etch every feature of his face in my memory and save it in my head forever.

Phones help. I slowly turned it to silent mode and clicked a few pictures of Tushar for the future, before putting the phone away to take advantage of the present. I could never get enough of looking at him. And it was a very good opportunity, one that I could not miss. Staring at a person when he's awake might

get kind of embarrassing after a while, but if the guy is asleep
. . . *jackpot!* You can stare at him all you want and he would not
even know how stupidly you are in love with him.

About two hours later, I struggled with keeping my eyelids
open. Being a vampire seemed like a good idea, if only for their
ability to stay up all night. My body was tired and crying for
sleep, my mind was drained and exhausted, just begging to be
put to rest, but my heart . . . oh no! It had still not had enough
of Tushar. I could stare at him all night. God knew how long
that relationship would last. I would want it to be forever . . .
but, it was not in my hands. I just vowed to make the most of
it whenever I had a chance.

I was distracted by my phone blinking. There was a text
from Vatsala.

*Vatsala: It's awesome again! Because I LOVE Ankit. I LOVE
LOVE LOVE him!*

Chhavi: Good for you!

Vatsala: Didn't tell him about Ronit yet . . .

Chhavi: Relax. Take your time. What's the rush?

Vatsala: Actually . . . I forgot to mention before . . .

Chhavi: What?

Vatsala: I have to meet Ronit again. For a longer time. Alone.

Chhavi: WHAT??

*Vatsala: Yeah . . . there's this slot in MTV he wanted to talk to me
about . . .*

Chhavi: Oh. Work-related! Phew.

Vatsala: Yeah . . . I'm nervous . . .

Chhavi: I know.

Vatsala: Am I a bad person?

Chhavi: NO! Are you kidding me?! You're great. I love you!!!

*Vatsala: Hehe! I think I'll tell Ankit about it tomorrow. I can't meet
Ronit before telling Ankit first . . .*

Chhavi: Good idea! Don't worry, he'll understand . . .

Vatsala: Hmmm . . . Anyway, how's it going with you guys?
Chhavi: Great!
Vatsala: Am I disturbing?
Chhavi: No, he's asleep.
Vatsala: Don't tell me you're sitting there watching him sleep!
Chhavi: What if I was?
Vatsala: It would totally creep me out!
Chhavi: You're just plain weird.
Vatsala: I know.
Chhavi: Haha!
Vatsala: Chal, I'll go sleep now. Have a shoot tomorrow . . .
Chhavi: Oh, yeah! Okay, go!
Vatsala: Night! Wake Tushar up and have some hot nasty sex. It's better than staring at a sleeping him, trust me!
Chhavi: Yeah, yeah!
Vatsala: Really, you're wasting precious time.
Chhavi: You think?
Vatsala: Yep! He'll be gone tomorrow . . .
Chhavi: Hmm . . . I think I will wake him up, after all!
Vatsala: Clever!
Chhavi: See ya!

Just for the record—I did *not* wake him up that night. He looked too cute asleep. And you can't really stare at your guy's face once the hot and heavy make out starts.

I Think I Love You!

The next two weeks were hell. *Hell.* Staying away from Tushar had never been more difficult than this. The minutes passed so, *so* slowly. And even though I didn't really have time to even think about him, that was the only thing I did all day, all night long. *Think about him. Dream of him.* With every breath I took.

There was no other way to it. In the beginning, I did try to involve myself in work and forget about him. But it just would not happen. He would not stay off my mind. All I did those days was move around the house like a lovesick lunatic. I even had that dreamy look in my eyes.

Naitik had not yet turned out to be the magician everyone had implied he was. He was not really pulling good modelling offers out of the thin air. So, there was no work yet. But there would be—Naitik had assured me. He was doing stuff to take care of that. Until that happened, the only thing I had to work on was the small sports slot I did for Metro News.

'Please don't schedule anything for the next three days,' I told Naitik over phone.

'Why so? Going for a weekend trip in the middle of the week, babes?'

'No! Tushar is coming . . .'

'And he has asked you to spend every single second of your next three days with him?' he shot.

'No. I want to.'

'Oh, man. Fuck this love. You know why God ever thought of creating such a thing as love? To screw my life. All my clients seem to have fallen in love at the same time!'

'And it affects you how?' I asked.

'Are you freaking kidding me? If my clients do not take up projects, I do not get my commission. And my girlfriend doesn't get her latest demand fulfilled. Because of which, *I do not get laid*. And that, I tell you, is *very* bad for my mental and physical health.'

I laughed. I liked Naitik a lot. He was always so full of all kinds of bullshit!

'So, babes, the more you work, the better it is for the peace of my mind and of what twitches inside my boxers. Bring your cute butt back to work soon. And send me some videotapes of the awesome sex you are planning to have.'

I hung up.

Tired of meeting in bars and hotel rooms every time he was in town, we had decided to meet at Marine Drive that day. He had suggested it and I had jumped at the chance. Meeting him in the daytime sometimes would do good to the future of our relationship. And I was definitely looking for something more substantial and more long-term. So I wanted to meet sometimes without make-outs in the picture.

I waited for him, looking out at the wide span of water that stretched in front of me. Marine Drive had always been my most favourite place in Mumbai. It was the best remedy for getting over the low feeling whenever I had it. The feelings of restlessness and hopelessness that often seemed to take over me in drastic situations had no other solution. I had always loved taking a walk there in the evenings. But I had always been alone.

And it sucked.

Even though I had been pretty content with the relationship I had with Tushar till then, I wanted more. A lot more. At first, I had not minded entering a non-serious relationship. I had not been a relationship with anyone for some time then, and was not looking to get into one either. So I had thought having a physical relationship would be enough.

But then I started to like Tushar. And eventually, love came into the picture, like it always does. And I *knew* he was in love with me too. Everything he did or said implied so. Just that he didn't realize it. So, I had decided to wait for him to realize it on his own. I was in no rush. Or maybe I was. It was just that—I was getting good at hiding it.

'Hey,' he whispered in my ear and came to stand next to me.

'Hi,' I smiled as I turned to look at him.

Every time I looked at him, the first thought that inevitably came to my mind was—*Man! How can someone be so handsome?* And that day was no exception. But seeing him in the broad daylight brought with it some revelations too. The light in the bars and the hotel rooms weren't enough to highlight the colour of his eye. They were an exotic shade of chocolate brown. I was relieved; for some reason, guys with light coloured eyes always scare me.

As I looked at him and evaluated if he was good boyfriend material, I realized how stupid it was of me. I was already hopelessly in love with the guy, had slept with him a few times, and was only just now checking if he was datable!

Still, it was nice to notice his facial features. They were as appealing directly under the sun as they were under those neon lights we were generally exposed to. The warm, twinkling eyes, the straight nose, the amazing lips, the boyish grin. And every single strand of his hair, even though ruffled, seemed to fall exactly at the right place.

That day, his stubble suggested that he hadn't shaved in the past couple of days. That only added to his charm and made him look even sexier. Even though I had been up for hours at a row to stare at him, I realized that all that was still not enough. I could stare at him for *centuries*. I guess being a vampire would have been a good idea after all.

'So, what's up? Have you been waiting long?' he asked.

'No. Just fifteen minutes or so. I don't mind, though. I like it here. It's so calm and serene.'

'Yeah. It's a nice place to meet,' he replied, turning to look at the sea.

'You think so? Is it better than the bar, then?'

He thought about it for a moment before replying, 'It depends . . . on what follows. As long as we are going to bed together later, every place is awesome to me.'

'Jerk,' I said as he grinned.

'What? Am I not supposed to want you?'

'You are supposed to want me. But not *all the time*.'

'You don't like it?' he asked.

I looked up at him. Don't like it? What girl won't like it if a guy like him wants her? *A girl who wants him to want her for a lot more than just physical reasons*, came a voice from inside. Obviously, I silenced it and said, instead, 'Are you kidding me? I love it.'

'So, that means I am getting laid after this?'

I smiled a fake smile and turned to look at the sea again. So, this is how it was going to be like. He was still not going to acknowledge his feelings for me, we were still going to keep it purely physical and I was going to have to walk along the Marine Drive alone, *forever*.

'Let's walk?' I asked, not wanting to miss this one chance I had of having some company for my walk along Marine Drive for once.

'Sure,' he said and we started walking. For the first fifteen minutes, we didn't say anything. I wondered what he was thinking. I, for one, was just capturing everything that was happening and saving it for ever in my mind. I was not going to have any more of it again, so I had better cherish it while I was still getting it.

'We have three days together,' Tushar said after a while.

'Yes, we do. Planning on spending it all in bed, are you?' Although I wanted him to say *no*, I knew he would say *yes*. But I could not blame him for that. Because, after all, that was what our relationship was all about—sex. Loads of it. *And just that.* Crap.

'Every guy's dream, eh?' he winked.

I didn't say anything. For some reason, I suddenly wanted to run away and never come back. Which girl in her right mind would ever agree to have an open relationship with a guy like Tushar? Didn't I just *know* I would fall for him? And didn't he already say he didn't have time to get into a serious relationship at the moment? Then why did I have to agree to this? Why did I *have* to invite the pain?

I had been stressed over the last few days. I had spent nights up, wondering what the future held for the two of us. When would Tushar realize that he loved me? And when would we have a real relationship, if ever? I had no answers to those questions.

Then, as I walked with him along the sea, it suddenly hit me that he would probably never realize he loved me. And so, we would never really be together like an actual couple. I had already been scared and by that time, I had reached paranoia. There was a slight constriction in my throat and I was worried I might cry.

'Chhavi? Is everything okay?' His voice brought me back to present.

'Yeah, everything is fine,' I looked at him and smiled.

'You are in some other world today. You look very lost.'

'No, I was just thinking . . .'

'About?' he asked.

'Work,' I said automatically. I was never going to tell him anything about how I feel. I didn't want to complicate things. Okay. Truth—I was just scared to death about how he would respond to that. There was a very good chance that by demanding commitment I might scare him away.

'Oh. Things are going fine at work?'

'Kind of. The only interesting thing I have going is the five minute sports slot. Other than that, offers aren't exactly pouring in.'

'Really? Even with Naitik? He could not bring in good projects?' he asked.

'Nothing really interesting. Just the same old boring advertisements.'

'Things will come up. He will do something. Don't worry,' he said reassuringly. Everyone who knew Naitik had complete confidence in him. Initially, it used to amaze me, but then I got used to it. And it also helped in boosting my confidence, seeing Naitik so aggressive and dynamic around the clock. And slowly, I had come to believe—as long as I had Naitik with me, nothing could go wrong.

'I hope so. Naitik will work something out,' I said.

It was almost dark by then and the lights had been turned on. And I tell you—at night, when Marine Drive is illuminated by those countless lights, the place looks absolutely stunning. When you stand there and look out at the sea, you inevitably feel insignificant. You realize how big the world is and how small your existence is.

But right then, the only thing killing me was my insignificance in Tushar's life.

'So, what do you want to do next?' Tushar turned to me and asked as we made our way out.

'Whatever you say . . .'

'I say . . .' he thought for a minute. 'Let's do something to cheer you up.'

I shook my head. '*Naah!* It is just one of my moods. I will be okay in a while.'

'One of your moods, is it? So, I will just have to learn how to deal with *all* of your moods . . . Now that I am going to spend so much time with you, it would be easier if I understood you better.'

'Huh? We are going to spend more time together?' I asked, confused. *What was he talking about? Was he talking about what I hoped he was talking about?* My heartbeat rose.

'Obviously,' he made a face. *What was so obvious about it?*

'Tushar.'

'Chhavi.'

'Don't play with me,' I looked down at the sand and said.

'I am not playing. I mean it. I really do intend to spend more time with you.'

'In bed?'

'Yes.'

I gave him a stare. It was not very effective, though. The deadly look I had intended on giving him came out all wrong. I was too close to tears, which totally ruined the intensity of my stare.

'And on the couch. And the shower. And the table top. And the el—Hey!' he held my arm as I turned to leave. I protested and tried to run, but it didn't work. He was too strong. I knew. I had been with him quite a few times.

'Let me go,' I looked down and said. I didn't look into his eyes. I didn't want him to see the hurt there.

'Come on! You know I was just fooling around.'

'*Don't* fool around! Didn't I tell you already—Do. Not. Play. With. Me.' And to my intense embarrassment, the tears I had been holding back all this while chose to suddenly start flowing down my cheek. I wanted to run away, but he still had a hold on me.

'Chhavi, no. Please don't cry.' He held my arms and pulled me close.

'No,' I said and pulled away. 'I don't want to do this anymore. Things have changed. And this . . . this *thing* we have is *not* working for me anymore.'

'You think I don't see that? You think I am blind?'

I looked up at him, puzzled. *He knew?*

'I know this isn't working for you anymore. And I know it isn't working for *me* either.'

I stayed silent.

'Don't cry. Please.'

I sniffed and wiped away the tears from my cheek.

'Chhavi . . . I know this is difficult for you. But trust me—it has been equally difficult for me too. Even more, I think. You are a girl, so you are good at dealing with your emotions. While I . . . this is all new to me.'

'*What* is new to you?' I asked softly.

'This. Us. It isn't still just an open relationship, is it? I can never imagine seeing you with another guy. And I know you cannot see me with some other girl. It was written in bold all over your face at that reception that night,' he smiled.

I blushed red.

'So why pretend anymore? Let's say it outright—I want more.'

I couldn't believe it was happening. I couldn't believe it was *actually* happening. He was actually saying all that. He was actually acknowledging that there was something more than just the physical chemistry between us.

'Say something,' he said.

'I don't know what to say. Why do you want more?'

'Because . . . I think I love you,' he looked into my eyes and said seriously.

I was stunned. I stared at him for three whole minutes, before a smile crept onto my face slowly and I said, 'I think I love you too.'

The next three days were, after all, spent in bed.

~

'So you never really knew your parents?' I asked Tushar. We had gone to watch a movie, but it turned out to be so boring that we ended up talking to each other instead. Or maybe it was just us. We enjoyed each other's company too much to care about a stupid movie and waste our precious and measured time in it.

And Tushar was acting kind of weird that day. I had just randomly asked where his parents were when he said, 'I have no parents.' At first, I thought he was kidding. But then he told me that he had not really lived with his parents ever. And that his Dad died when he was a kid.

I instantly regretted bringing the topic up. He was all pensive and serene the whole day. I had never seen him like that. It was as if there was this whole new angle to him that I had never known. It was hardly something to be amazed about, as I did not know him that well. But I was starting to. And I realized that there was much more to him than what he let on.

'No,' he shook his head and said. 'Mom and Dad separated when I was only nine . . .'

'And your custody was given to . . .?'

'Dad,' he said and I saw a small smile creep up on his face.

'You loved him, didn't you?' I asked.

He didn't say anything, but his expression said it all. That trace of a smile he had on his face was enough to tell me everything I needed to know.

'How did he . . .?' I asked.

'Car accident. I was there in the car with him . . . I saw him bleed to death . . . in front of my eyes . . .'

He had a distant look in his eyes. His eyes changed a little colour, and I realized it must have something to do with his mood. And I could see the shine of tears there. It broke my heart to see him like that. He looked like the nine year old kid he was when his father died. He looked lost.

I held his hand and squeezed it. He looked away.

'I'm sorry,' I whispered.

He nodded.

After that, we didn't bring up the topic again. We didn't even talk to each other till the movie ended. I kept stealing glances at him, to see if he was okay. He kept ignoring me, looking at everything other than me.

It was later that night, when we were having dinner together, that he brought it up again. 'You know, it wasn't like I was the only child in the world who didn't have a dad. But losing him somehow was like losing the entire family . . .'

'Why? What about your mom? She didn't take you back?'

'No.'

I waited for him to say something. I wanted to know, but decided not to prod.

At last, he sighed and said, 'After Mom and Dad separated, Dad was still trying to fix things with her. He was trying to make the marriage work . . . for my sake. But Mom was totally against the idea. She wouldn't listen to anything he said.'

'Was there someone else?' I asked slowly, weighing my words.

'I think so. I never knew the reason behind their separation. I still don't. But I guess it was her decision . . . and some other man in her life . . . Dad tried his best to convince her to come back. He didn't want that one . . . one . . . *incident* to affect our lives so much,' he said.

'He was willing to forgive her and take her back?'

'Yes. But forgiveness was not what she wanted. She wanted something else—a divorce.'

'Shit.' The word left my mouth before I could stop it. I bit my tongue.

To my surprise, Tushar met my eye and a tiny smile played at the ends of his lips.

'Sorry,' I murmured meekly.

'Never mind,' he said and continued in a very mechanical tone, speaking really fast. It was as if he was eager to get over and done with the story as quickly as possible. 'So, she didn't want to get back with him. Because she was in "love" with that other man.' He spat out the word *love* as if it was something that disgusted him. 'And so, when they got a divorce, Dad got my custody. More like—she *gave* Dad my custody. And married that man. Dad died a little later.'

'She didn't come back for you?'

'Oh, yes. She did come back. For the funeral. But not for me. She left after the two hour formality.'

'Where did you go then? Where did you stay?' I asked.

'Relatives. They took turns, letting me stay with them out of pity.'

'Tushar . . .' I wanted him to stop. I could not bear to listen to it anymore. I could not even begin to imagine how he went through all that, at such a young age.

'And then, I came across this really unique, vintage camera.

It was Dad's. He wasn't really interested in photography, but he must have bought it in some auction or something. And I clicked random pictures . . . just to pass time. Then I started sending them to various magazines . . . One day, I hit jackpot.'

'And that's how it all started,' I smiled.

'Yes. And that is why I don't have a home. That is why I choose to live a nomad's life.'

'Because you lived like that when you were a kid?'

'Because you need a family to have a home,' he said.

I wanted to ask if he met his Mom after that. Or if he wanted to see her now. And did they talk over the phone. I wanted to know if he was still in touch with his relatives who he had once lived with. And I wanted to ask if he will have a home, when he has a family. Or was he too sore to take the risk. I wanted to be his family. I wanted to create a home with him.

But I didn't say anything. He was already too disturbed. As I looked at him in between bites, I saw him meet my eyes and smile at me. The smile lacked happiness. His eyes were still a little sad.

It hurt, just to see him hurt.

Long Distance Sucks

'How are we going to do this?' I asked Tushar on the phone. It was so frustrating. He had not been in the city for a whole week and I was missing him terribly. And that was when we had spent those heavenly three days together. I had thought that they would be enough to last a fortnight, by when he would be back after his assignment. But it did not even last a week. If it was so bad in seven days, I did not want to think what my condition would be on the fourteenth. Life is so unfair.

'Do what?' he asked.

'Tushar, come on! How is this going to work if we do not even try to make it work?'

'We don't need to try! Things will go on as before. Nothing has changed . . .'

'What do you mean nothing has changed?' I asked.

'. . . has it?

'I . . .' I didn't know what to say. He said he loved me. And I said I loved him too. And we shared things about our past and stuff we had never told anyone else. And—I should finally tell you this now—the three days that we spent together were spent mostly in bed, yes. But they were not spent making love. We were just talking to each other. And it was amazing! We were in love!

And now, he was saying nothing had changed! How could everything be the same? How could we continue going on like before? Would it be the same now too? Would he call me whenever he was in Mumbai and we would meet up and have sex? Would we still not have any contact when he was not here?

Was it still just about the sex? *Is he out of his freaking mind?*

'Chhavi! Why are you worrying so much? We will still have what we had before. *Plus the love.* How can it get any better?'

'I don't think we are on the same page here . . .' I said, and wondered why he didn't sound worried in the least.

'So tell me what you're thinking then. Think aloud. Let's work on this together,' he said.

'I just . . . see—before that day, we were just . . . you know, using each other for sex, right?'

'Right,' he sounded amused.

'*What?* What's so funny? Are you laughing at me?'

'The way you put it—*using each other for sex*. It's funny,' he laughed.

'Tushar! Pay attention.'

'Oh. Alright. Tell me. I am listening.'

'So, we were just partners in bed and there were no strings attached. But now we are *more*. Now you have said you love me . . .' I smiled at the thought. *He loved me.* It was still not getting old. The thought still was enough to make my day. I could not say the same thing about my nights, though. They were not made. They were torturous.

'Yes. And you said you love me back. So we are in love with each other. So? Isn't that a *good* thing?'

'Yes, it is. But it also complicates everything. We don't live in the same city and—'

'I don't live in any city,' he interjected. I ignored him.

'—how are we supposed to have a relationship if we don't even meet? Meeting once a week is enough?'

'Oh, so you want to meet more? That's sweet!'

'Tushar!' I shouted.

'Okay, okay. I will be all serious and grave now. But I still don't see what the big issue is! I know that we don't live in the same city. And I know we cannot keep on like this forever. But this is just temporary. I am not going to be a nomad forever!'

'That is not what I meant. I wasn't thinking about *that* yet. Not that long term. Just that . . . it would be nice to meet more.'

'I know. And I want to have a real relationship too. But, we can't do anything about that *yet*, can we? So, let's look at this in a positive way. We will now have the amazing lovemaking *and* the love,' Tushar said.

'But this is all getting complicated. Now, with love in it . . .'

'You worry too much. We will meet as much as we used to. And now there will be mails and calls and texts too. And flowers and dates and candle-night dinners. And long drives and late night chats and . . . you get the idea?'

I smiled, 'Yes, I do. And now that you put it this way . . . it sounds AWESOME.'

'You see? I am a genius! And if you miss me too much . . . we can always try phone sex.'

'You wish! I will never do such a thing—'

He cut me off with, 'Why? It is great, I have heard. With all the dirty talk and—'

'Exactly. Do I look like someone who would talk dirty?'

'Oh, that is not an issue. I will do the talking. And you will catch up eventually . . .'

'Not going to happen. I would like torturing you, instead,' I teased.

'Will it be just me who would be tortured? Tell me that you will not miss me as much as I will miss you. Tell me that you will not cry yourself to sleep, every night I am away!'

'You are *so* delusional. And how do you want me to react? Shall I feed you sympathy?'

'You are my girlfriend now. The one person in the whole wide world who is supposed to play along with whatever I say. The person who is supposed to make me feel good about myself. So is a little sympathy too much to expect?' he asked. And he sounded so cute that I just wanted to give him a big hug. But then I remembered—he was not in the same city. Shit. Okay stop. No negative thought. I put on a smile.

'Aww. Of course not! I would be *distraught* if we do not have sex on the phone. I mean, how will I go through night after night without your sexy talks? In fact, you do not even need to talk dirty. Just your voice would be enough. The way you speak . . . and the texture of your voice would be enough to drive me to . . . the *apex* of . . . *undying* pleasure.'

He didn't say anything.

'Tushar? Are you there? Why are you suddenly so silent?' I asked.

'I was thinking . . . Why did God have to make me so perfect? You girls fall so madly in love with me . . .'

'How true! It is an unfair world, isn't it?'

'Exactly. Umm . . . I was thinking . . . since you are so excited about the whole idea of doing it over the phone, let's do a rehearsal now! I will start,' he said. His voice suddenly turned huskier, as he asked, 'So, what are you wearing right now?'

'Tushar . . .'

'No, don't say anything. Let me guess. The green bra? The one with small black hearts all over it?'

'Tushar!' I shouted.

'No? Then, the beige one? With the hot pink laces on it? Oh, I *so* love that one. The way it cups you, and the way it makes your cleav—'

'Oh boy! You are serious about this!'

'Of course. I want to discuss every detail of what covers your assets and how perfectly. Did I sound like I was kidding?' he asked.

'No. But I didn't think it would work!'

'It is working? Already? I did not even start properly yet. I was just thinking about how your nipp—'

'Hey, Tushar, I will have to call you back,' I said.

'Why? Reached it already?'

'No, I am serious. It's Vatsala. I think she has been crying.'

'Is something wrong?' he asked.

'I am not sure . . . there was something . . . but I thought it was sorted. Anyway. Long story. Call you back?' I asked.

'Sure. Take care, of both of you.'

'Love you. Bye.'

~

'Oh, come on, Vatsala. Open the door,' I called from the living room for the millionth time. Her room had been locked since the morning and I had been waiting for her to open it but she had not come out of it even once. I had been dying to tell her all about Tushar and me, and to share my insecurities about our long-distance relationship, but she seemed to be sleeping more than usual. So I had not disturbed her. Never once had it occurred to me that something might be wrong with her. Things were perfect just a few days ago, weren't they?

It was when I was on the phone with Tushar when I saw her come out of her room, to get some water. I noticed that something was wrong. The puffed eyes and the red nose said it all. But by the time I hung up, she locked herself up in her room again.

'Vatsala! Would you just open the bloody door already?'

'Go away,' came a muffled response from the other side of the door.

'But why? What have I done?'

'I want to be left alone.' Her voice was clearer this time.

'But I will not leave you alone. I want to know what is wrong.'

'I cannot tell you. It is personal.'

'What? Don't I know everything about you already? How can it be personal, then?' I asked.

'It's just . . . something I can't express . . . And you will judge.'

'I won't.'

'You will give me a long, exhausting lecture,' she said.

'I won't.'

'Promise?'

'Promise.'

There was a brief pause after which the door was unlocked. I turned the knob and pushed the door open. Vatsala was standing in the room, with her back to me. And she didn't turn when I entered.

'What is wrong?' I asked, keeping my distance from her. She was that type of a girl. When she was sad, she would prefer talking about it to someone, but from a distance. I don't think she had ever held hands or hugged someone when feeling low.

'Take a wild guess . . .'

I didn't have to. I knew. It is always the same. 'Ronit Oberoi? What happened?'

'I am meeting him tomorrow.'

'I know. And I also know that you haven't told Ankit about it? Do you plan to?'

'Eventually,' she answered.

'And this is what is bothering you? Going to see Ronit without telling Ankit about it?'

'Hmmm . . .'

'Vatsala, don't give yourself such a hard time about it. It is not a *date*, it is a *meeting*. It is *work*,' I said.

'Actually . . .' she left off and met my eye. Her swollen eyes said it all.

'Oh God. It is *not* work related, is it? Then what is it? And *why*?'

'I don't know. He asked me to meet him and I could not say no. *I just could not.* He is *Ronit*. How could I say no?'

'But why lie to *me* about it? You could have just said that you were going to see him because you wanted to,' I said.

'It is not like that. I had not planned on it. He just . . . When we met, we got talking. Then . . . he said he would like to see me sometime. And we were free this Friday, so we set a meeting.'

'There is no other reason? Nothing related to work? You said something about some slot on MTV?'

'He did say something about it . . . just casually, meaning he would like it if I work with his channel and stuff . . .' she said.

'Oh man. This is so screwed. Don't go,' I said. I could think of no other way to deal with the situation.

'But I want to meet him,' she said in a very low voice. I had never heard Vatsala use that tone. She sounded so devastated.

'You cannot have it all. And Ankit? Do I need to tell you how lucky you are to have him? Will you ever find someone like him again? Will Ronit ever care for you the way Ankit does?'

She stayed silent.

'No, Vatsala. He will not. No one can. The way Ankit loves you . . .'

'But I love him too! You *know* I love Ankit.'

'And that's exactly what I mean! I *know* how much you love

each other. So where does Ronit fit in your story? Don't meet him. It will wreck everything.'

'But . . . I don't know what it is about Ronit . . . I just cannot *not* like him. I just . . .'

'I understand, Vatsala. Trust me, I really do. But . . .' I shook my head.

'Oh shit,' she closed her eyes and sighed.

'You can't have it all. And leaving Ankit for Ronit . . . leaving Ankit for *anyone* . . . it just doesn't make sense.'

'I will never leave Ankit,' she shook her head vigorously and said.

'I will never let you.'

'I am not going,' she said. Her voice had enough conviction to make me heave a sigh of relief.

I smiled.

Ground Rules

'Holy shit!' I exclaimed as I let Tushar in my apartment. I did not know he was coming. And I loved surprises. Especially when they were *that* good. He was the best surprise I could ever get. And I could not wait to unwrap my present.

He hugged me and we kissed. Gosh! I had missed him so much. That day, his face was not covered with that stubble. But he still managed to look equally breath-taking. We were just about to take it to full-fledged snogging when I heard Vatsala clear her throat.

'Hey Vatsala,' Tushar said as we broke the embrace.

'Hi,' she said shortly and turned to me, 'Have you told Tushar? About Ronit?'

'No, I haven't.'

'Can I talk to you for a minute then? In private?'

'Okay, sure,' I said and turned to Tushar, 'Just a second?'

'Of course. Take your time,' he smiled.

I followed Vatsala into her room, wondering what this was all about. Ronit, no doubt, but what? Had she decided to go meet him, after all?

'Something happened,' she said, once we were inside the room.

'Umm . . . are you going to see him?' was what came out of my mouth. That was what I cared about the most at the minute. I could not let that happen. I could not let Vatsala ruin what she had with Ankit. Not if I could help it.

'No,' she laughed dryly.

I let out a sigh of relief. 'What is it, then?' I asked.

'I received a mail from Ronit. See . . .'

I'm sorry I can't make it today. Things came up. Some other time?

'Oh. So, isn't this good? It makes things easier for you. Now you won't have to cancel,' I said.

'Chhavi . . . he doesn't want to see me.'

'It doesn't look so. He "can't make it today" because "things came up" and he said that he wants to see you "some other time" . . .'

'That is all just an excuse. Just to be polite,' she said sadly.

'Vatsala, I am sure he meant what he said. And even if he did not, how does it matter?'

'You don't get it! No one gets it! *He doesn't want me.*'

I could see that she was hurt. And I could see that she felt insulted, but I didn't see *why*. So what if a guy doesn't want to see her. It happens all the time. Some guys are into you, some guys aren't. This is how it is. You just have to deal with it.

'I don't know what to say,' I said honestly.

'Go to your boyfriend. He is waiting. I know you don't have any time for me anymore.'

'Oh, come on. You know it is not like that. Yes, he is my boyfriend and I love him and I want to be with him . . . especially because we are together for such short periods of time. But that definitely does *not* mean I care about you any "less".'

'I am sorry. I didn't mean to hurt you . . . it is just that, you don't understand all this. You don't know how important this is for me,' she said and looked up at me with her big brown baby-like eyes. She was just a kid.

'Yes, I do *not* understand. Last night, we decided that you will not go. *You* said you will not go. That you would never leave Ankit—'

'I won't leave Ankit! I will never leave him! I still stand by that.'

'So, you will not leave Ankit and you still will not let Ronit go either? It does not happen like this. You *cannot* have them both together,' I shouted. I was frustrated by now.

'But Ronit—'

'We have already discussed this, Vatsala. Ronit's chapter is closed. Let it be. He cancelled, and you weren't going anyway. So what is the big deal?'

'You don't know how it is to feel rejected,' she barely whispered.

'I don't? You think there is a single person on the planet that has not been rejected even once in life?'

'Not by the same person. Over and over again.'

'*Especially* by the same person. Because that one person doesn't like you. He never did, he never will. So it is obvious that he will reject you every time,' I reasoned.

'But it hurts.'

'Of course it hurts! It is supposed to hurt! That is precisely why you need to forget all about it. And forget all about him.'

'But—' she started again.

'*No buts!* For the last time, Vatsala—MOVE ON. This is not fair to Ankit,' I shouted, finally losing my calm. 'If you go on like this, you are going to lose him. And for what? This is sheer stupidity. I don't know *what is wrong with you.*'

She stayed silent for a moment. I thought she was pissed. I have never shouted at her like that. Hell, I have never shouted at *anyone* like that. But she was being so difficult to deal with, I had no other option.

When she turned, she had a funny look on her face that I
could not read. I told you—she never repeats an expression.
So it becomes really difficult to read her face sometimes. 'Go,'
she said.

'What?'

'Go to Tushar.'

'See, Vatsala . . . I didn't mean to offend—' I started to
apologize.

'I am not offended. I am happy. It felt nice. No one shouts
at me.'

I laughed and shook my head, 'For a moment there, you
scared me. And of course no one shouts at you. You scare people
away. They won't shout at you unless they are close to you.'

'I like it that you consider me *close* enough to shout at me,'
she said.

'Aww,' I smiled.

'You know, a few nights ago, I had this dream about you
. . . and me. You know, a lesbian fantasy . . .'

'*What?*'

'And I would really like to get all *close* to you right here right
now, but with your boyfriend in the next room, it would be
weird,' she made a face.

'Umm . . . I think I should go.'

'Oh wait. It might not be weird. If we could invite him to
join us . . .'

I turned on my heels and left.

~

'You really like this, don't you?' I asked Tushar.

'I really like what?'

'This. Your life. Career. Photography.'

'I enjoy what I do, yes. Photography is something I have

always had fervour for. And the glam that follows is obviously very attractive too,' he answered.

'The glam . . . you got it all at the age of, what? Sixteen?'

'Seventeen. And it was accidental. I told you, I had shot those photos purely out of interest. Never thought they would create such a buzz.'

'I remember reading something about it on the net,' I confessed.

'And you came across it how?' he asked, looking amused.

'I Googled you,' I met his eye and replied seriously.

'That's kind of flattering,' he grinned.

'*Naah!* I was just acting like a true girlfriend. Keeping tabs. Digging into background stories. Searching for hidden skeletons . . . the usual stuff, you know?'

'Oh! Any luck yet?'

'As of now—no. But I won't give up. I *will* search for something to nag you about later,' I said.

'Sure. We should try fighting sometime. It would feel like a real relationship then. Right now, it is just all too sweet.'

'It is the honeymoon phase. Will end soon, though. And then we will have huge battles. All swords and sandals.'

'Swords?' he laughed.

'Oh, you will—' I stopped mid-sentence as his phone started ringing. He looked at it uncertainly. 'Go on. Pick it up,' I prodded.

'Hello?' he said on the phone.

He got busy talking on the phone and I looked around myself. We were at the Powai Lake that day. We had taken the meeting-in-the-daytime thing too seriously and thought exploring the city would be a good change from dance bars. And I liked it too.

I do not remember the place very well, as I had spent my time *engrossed* in other things. Namely, Tushar. But I remember feeling nice when I was there. Or maybe it was just Tushar. He had that effect on me; I always felt nice, when I was with him.

It had been a month since we had started dating. And it had been running very smoothly. The first three days we spent together were followed by fifteen days of no-see. After which he had surprised me by coming to see me. And then, it was the second time he had done that. And I loved him for it. He was really trying to make this work, especially because I was so worried that it might not.

'I really cannot help you with this right now,' I heard him say on the phone. He sounded stressed.

I raised my eyebrows, to which he shook his head. And tiptoed his fingers to at not-so-decent places of my body.

'Listen, I apologize for cancelling at the last minute, but trust me, I had no other option. Something came up and I had to go,' he said sternly, paused for a minute and said, 'I understand. Sure. Okay,' and hung up.

Though I wanted to, I did not ask who it was. That would have sounded so girlfriend-ish. But then my curiosity got the better of me and I asked, 'Who was that?'

'A client. I had to cancel on him today.'

'To come here?'

He shrugged. 'It wasn't that great a project anyway.'

'But you had a deal with him. You can't cancel like that at the last minute.'

'I wanted to meet you,' he said, looking at me.

'I know you did. And I really love you for that but—' He didn't let me complete.

'So I should get a reward for coming, right? You said you love me for this. So, would you *show* me how much you appreciate the gesture?'

'Tushar.'

'Yes, baby?' he smiled sweetly at me.

I laughed and went a little red in the face, 'All this won't work on me. Don't—'

'I think it already is . . . it is working quite well on you,' he grinned. He had taken to teasing me mercilessly about my *Excessive Blushing Syndrome*.

I tried to maintain a stern face, 'Stay on the topic. You have to concentrate on your career. You cannot—'

'Yes, I can. I can fly here to see you whenever I want to. Because I love you and I am taking this seriously.'

'You don't have to make your work suffer just to make this work. If we love each other enough, which I am sure we do, it will work itself out.'

'You don't want me to make an effort?'

'No, it's not like that. I love you for making the effort. But . . .'

'I love you too.'

'. . . not at the cost of your career. I won't let you sabotage your career because of this.' I finished, ignoring what he said in between.

'Oh, come on. It is just one assignment. It would hardly sabotage my career.'

'So, you won't do this again then?'

'I can't promise that. What? Don't look at me like that. I love you. I want to spend time with you. And skipping a few unimportant assignments won't affect my career,' he said.

'And cancelling at last moment, with no prior notice, won't this affect your image?'

He looked at me wordlessly for ten full seconds before saying, 'You worry too much. We will take it as it comes. It is all about priorities. You should be happy that I put you at that top rank in the list.'

'I *am* happy. It's just—'

'Hush. You're wasting precious time. We should establish some ground rules, you know?'

'We should? Like?' I asked.

'Like we will save all the nagging and the complaining for when we are not together. We will do it over phone calls or mails. So, Ground Rule 1—*When we are together, we concentrate exclusively on the physical things.* No nagging in person. The better things, we will do when we meet. Things that we cannot do over the phone or the internet . . .'

'I can see where this is going . . .' I hid a smile.

'You do? I was just talking about holding hands, hugging each other, looking at each other up close, having a meal together . . .'

'Yeah, yeah. I'm sure you meant that.'

'Smart, you've always been! Anyway, jokes apart. Tell me— how do you like my plan?'

'Umm . . . it kind of does make sense . . . especially after that phone call of yours, when you were talking so sternly. Man, was it hot!'

'Ah! Was it? Anyway, see? I told you. We just need to manage stuff like I say and we will be awesome. I have more brilliant ideas in store. Wanna listen?'

And I listened. And they definitely made sense. And were quite interesting too. He held my hand and ran his fingers on the inside of my palm, as he whispered sweet nothings into my ear. He made me blush, he made me laugh and he made me shiver in anticipation. It was very romantic.

Powai Lake is a public place. We had to get out of there. And *soon.*

Ground Rule 2—*No more public places.*

Red Hot Pants

Twenty days. Twenty nightmarish days it had been since we had met. I was losing it. I was missing him like crazy and was going a little mad thinking about him. I was on the verge of doing something. Something bad.

But that wouldn't get me Tushar, would it?

I had no idea how people survived in a long distance relationship. There were couples who actually didn't meet for years! I was going mad in just twenty days. I simply did not have the kind of will power and patience, or whatever it is people need to maintain—and be happy in—a long distance relationship. It hurt, just thinking about the miles that separated us.

I got to be in his arms just once or twice in a month. And that was already too much for me to take. In those moments, I really did consider consulting some friend who had been doing long distance. Or maybe a shrink. I was not kidding when I said I was going a little crazy.

'Are you listening to what I am saying?' Naitik's stern voice jerked me back to reality.

'Huh? Yes . . . yes, of course,' I stammered.

He sighed. 'Why aren't you fucking taking this seriously?'

'I am,' I said automatically.

'No, you're not. We both know that. This is important, and you are not even paying attention.'

'Okay. Now I'm listening. And I'm serious. You were saying . . .?'

'Take this up. This doesn't pay well and it doesn't have glam attached, but it's decent. Take it,' he said.

'Naitik, it is cooking oil.'

'I know. So what? A-grade stars are doing dishwashing bar ads today. What is the big fucking deal?'

'A-grade stars, who are A-grade no more, you mean,' I said.

'How does it fucking matter? It is not anything insanely embarrassing, it pays okay, and the advertising company they are hiring is not that bad either. I do not see an issue here. Why are we even discussing this?' he let out, clearly frustrated.

'Listen to yourself, Naitik! A month ago, you were saying even toothpaste was not do-able, even when it was a multi-national brand. Now you want me to do cooking oil, that too one no one has ever heard of. Will they even air the advertisement?'

'It was a month ago. Things were looking good then.'

'And now?' I asked, already biting my nails in my mind. Not in real, though. I had got a manicure just the previous day.

'I won't lie to you, Chhavi . . . offers are not coming our way. I am trying everything, I am pulling every string. I have made you visible in the market. But somehow, offers just are not coming.'

'Is there a reason?'

'Not one I can understand. I have been working in this industry for almost fifteen years now. I started young, and I learnt well. I can look at a model and tell if she is going to make it. And there is not a single fucking thing about you that says you won't,' he said.

I stayed silent, thinking.

'You have solid two years' experience to back you. Plus you still very much have that edge. You are young, you are slim. I don't know what is wrong with anything, then.'

'Can this be . . .' A sudden idea crossed my mind. 'Can this be *personal*? Like a row with a partner at a firm? You know—the firm that is advertising.'

'Well, I don't think so. Usually, the owners of the brand have nothing to do with the advertising department. They don't even know which advertising company is working for them. As long as you don't mess things up with the producer or the director, I don't think there should be any issue.'

'What if the partner is a powerful man?'

'How powerful?' he asked.

'Someone like . . .' I paused, dreading his reaction. '. . . Valli?'

'*VALLI*? You mean . . . you mean Valli, the owner of . . .' he trailed off, shaking his head in disbelief.

'I—'

'Don't,' he raised his palm to stop me. 'I can't listen. I can't even *begin* to tell you the kind of contacts that man has. He is like a giant spider. His web spreads everywhere. Every-*fucking*-where.'

I stood at a corner of the room and looked away, deciding to let him cool down first. It wouldn't be any good telling him anything at that minute anyway. He seemed too unstable to reason with. Ten whole minutes it took him to come back to normal. All the while, I stood there in the corner of his office, staring intently at a dome shaped showpiece sitting near the lamp.

'Begin,' he said at last.

'He was trying to get me to his place to—'

'No. Way. He is not of that *breed*. Been in the business for thirty five years now. No such case, ever.'

'But—' I tried to explain.

'Listen, babes. We agents know everything. He has never been known as the lusty kind. In fact—'

'He wanted me for his son, who had the hots for me. There was a scene. I accidently insulted him in front of the entire set. And then I walked out on the shooting.'

'When did this happen?' Naitik asked.

'Just about the time I hired you. A week before that, I guess. In fact, a few contracts were called off and it got me worried. That was the reason I went for you.'

'But offers were there before, weren't they? *After* you hired me. There were several offers initially, remember?'

'Yes, the ones you said were bad for my image,' I said.

'Yes, those. And then it stopped again. How? Did you do something to jog his memory?'

'I don't think so. I didn't even see him after that episode. Oh wait. I did see him a few weeks ago. At Tara's reception. He was there. But nothing happened. I just saw him across the hall, but then I had to go, so I left.'

'You did not even say *hi* to him?' he asked.

'No.'

'And did he see you?'

'Yes,' I said.

'And, please say *no* to this—did he see you see him?'

'Umm, *no*.'

'Really?' he asked.

'No, I was lying. You asked me to say *no*.'

'This is *not* a joke, Chhavi Mukharjee! And since you somehow do not seem to understand the gravity of the situation, let me tell you—this guy is a *monster*. He *eats* people. Not just their career. The people themselves too. He has the power to make your life so miserable, to cause so much damage, that you will not even give a second thought to something as mundane as your *career*. Because your primary concern would be your *life*. You won't even be able to fucking breathe properly. He would fuck you. And he would fuck you bad.'

I was stunned. Valli didn't seem this *lethal* when I was with him alone in the green room. I never thought he could be that powerful. Or revengeful. But if Naitik meant what he said, I was royally screwed. And even though Naitik was already quite friendly with the F-word, I think he was reaching a new record very soon with the outburst.

'Really?' I asked slowly.

'*Naah!* I was just fooling around with you! How can someone stop you from breathing?' he chuckled.

'For a moment there, I really couldn't breathe,' I let out a long breath.

'Only *I* have that kind of power. The power to *destroy* people. The power to *end* careers. Men weep when they see me coming. And women run to the nearest beauty clinic to get their boobs done,' he laughed wickedly.

'You have a very weird sense of humour. It wasn't even funny.'

'Ha! The truth is not supposed to be funny, babes! And don't worry. I will take care of this asshole Valli,' he said seriously. I mean, he looked serious; I had no idea if the expression was real or fake.

'Are you serious?' I asked.

'This time—yeah. I am very fucking serious,' he nodded, looking amused.

'But isn't Valli powerful?'

'You think *I* am not powerful? Now that I know who the enemy is, it will be a hell of a lot easier to get you out of this shit. If not for my straight sexual preferences, I would have ass-fucked Valli by now,' he thundered.

'Is it just a fragment of my imagination or do you actually look excited about this?'

'Like hell, I am excited. It has been a long time since some dickhead has attacked one of my clients. This is *war*. It will be fun. There will be mud and tears. It will be rape and gore.'

I just hoped he did not mean all that literally. Also—by then, I was completely grossed out at his choice of words.

~

'You told him?' Vatsala asked, as she stood in my room, looking at me pack.

'Yeah,' I said. 'Where are my red shorts?'

'In the laundry, I guess. Didn't you wear them it recently?'

'I don't know. But I need them now. Tushar loves them.'

'Red hot pants or blue jeans, I don't think it matters. You guys don't take much time getting out of your clothes, anyway,' she stated matter-of-factly.

'Come on! We've barely made out ever since we've gotten into this *real* relationship. We make out a lot less than you think we do. We have better things to do now. We love each other! And anyway, that doesn't mean I should not dress up.'

'You can, if you wish to. But I don't see the need.'

'Vatsala, I am going to see my boyfriend. We are meeting after twenty days. Isn't it obvious that I would dress up for him?' I asked.

'*Twenty days*, Chhavi. You won't have the dress you dressed up in, on your body even for even twenty *seconds*.'

'It is useless reasoning with you,' I said, as I picked up my things and stuffed them in my bag.

'Exactly. So tell me—why is this not a surprise? You are taking such pains to fly all the way to Bengaluru to see him, it might as well have been a surprise. It would have been an added bonus.'

'What if he hadn't been there? I wanted to make sure the trip doesn't go waste.'

'How romantic,' Vatsala mocked.

'Practical.'

'Whatever. Your call. Your boyfriend. By the way, it's a good thing you told him beforehand. At least you won't find him in bed with some other girl,' she shrugged casually.

I stopped in my tracks.

She threw her hands up in the air, 'Kidding, kidding.'

'I know. And I trust him. He would never cheat on me. He loves me.'

'He *says* he loves you. There is a big difference between the two.'

'Vatsala . . .'

'Alright, I'm sorry,' she smiled. 'I was just feeling ditched. You are leaving me alone here to go to see him . . .'

'Oh, it didn't occur to me. I am so—'

'Oh, shut up! Why do you have to worry so much about everything? I was just kidding.'

'I never know with you. You are so unpredictable,' I said and smiled.

'Hmm . . . now that you are so worried about me, I probably shouldn't hide this from you . . . Actually, I *do* feel a little ditched. You always knew how I feel about you. I mean. . . *us*.'

'Oh, please. Don't start about your lesbian fantasies again!'

'What? No! That is old news now . . .' she let it hang.

'So, what do you mean then?'

'Remember that day I mentioned the three of us doing it *together* . . .?'

'I'll see you,' I said, as I closed the door behind me.

~

'Tushar Mehra?' I asked the friendly looking man at the set. Even though I had been let in the set almost instantly, it was taking me ages to actually pinpoint Tushar.

'Tushar *ji*? *Wahan*,' the man pointed to the general direction of my left.

I stood there and squinted till I finally spotted him. Then I concentrated on making my way to him, dodging people who were moving haphazardly all around me. Pack up time is always the busiest. By the time I reached the place where I had seen him, he was lost again. I stood there and looked around, lost and confused, trying to look at all directions at once, when out of the blue, I saw him standing right in front of me, smiling.

'What took you so long?' he asked.

'I've been here since ages. Just couldn't find you.'

'Why didn't you try calling my number?'

'Oh,' I said. I wonder why it didn't strike me. Maybe because I was going mad with the anticipation of meeting him and my brain wasn't working properly. Just maybe.

The time we spent together was beyond awesome. The rest of the world ceased to exist. He was especially sweet to me all the time. I wondered why.

I was wearing my red hot pants.

The Unofficial Date

Vatsala Tells Her Story—I

I never intended to do this. This was not planned. I swear. I had made up my mind to close the Ronit chapter of my life. Forever, this time. But it doesn't work that way. Things don't usually go as planned, do they?

I had never planned on seeing Ronit face to face. After getting together with Ankit, I had not even given Ronit a second thought. Mostly because I knew what would happen if I gave him a second thought.

There is just something about Ronit . . . something that just keeps making me go back to him. No matter what he does, no matter how pissed I am at him, no matter how many times I curse him in my mind . . . I just keep loving him the way I have always done.

Yes, I agree this might not be the 'love' love. But just because it is not in the conventional form, it does not mean that it is not love. It is. It is our own personal flavour of it.

No one ever seems to understand this. Especially with Ankit in the picture. They all think that I am mad to even think of Ronit when I have Ankit with me. They are all big fans of Ankit. I know why—because he is awesome. I know, because I know him best. And I love him most.

Just because I love Ronit too, does not mean I do not love Ankit. I just have a big heart!

And it is not cheating. I don't know how anyone can even begin to think that if I love Ronit, I am cheating on Ankit. It is the most bizarre notion anyone can come up with. I mean, come on! If a girl has a boyfriend, isn't she allowed to love Brad Pitt too? Or does a girl stop dreaming about Shahrukh Khan after she marries?

You see my point? Ronit Oberoi has never been any less than Pitt or SRK to me. I have always loved him and I still loved him. (Let's not go into 'I will always love him' though. I am very unpredictable!)

But of course, there is a difference. Pitt does not know me. He does not reply to my messages ever (darn!) and he is not the one I accidently ran into a few weeks ago. He is not the one who asked me out. And when I decided to cancel, he was not the one who cancelled it first, just making me want it even more. There is just some connection between me and the forbidden things in my life. They always hold a special charm for me. Until I have them, I want them very desperately. But once I get them, I do not want them anymore.

So by taking the offer off the table, Ronit had made me want it even more. So, when the next time he asked, I simply could not say no. It was not my fault, really. He called me himself. And he apologized for cancelling before. And asked me out again. It was such a sweet gesture. How could I have said no to that?

How could I say no to anything he says?

It was well after the call, when the euphoria faded, that I realized what I had done. And I realized that if I went on a date with him, I would not have any excuse left to defend myself with 'it's not cheating' anymore. It would be cheating. And it would not be fair to Ankit. And Chhavi—however sweet she might be otherwise—would probably slit my throat to create a fountain of blood or hang me on the fan by my intestine or something.

'But Chhavi is not here. She is with Tushar, and she is not coming

back until after I come back from my date with Ronit.' My inner self is pretty evil, I tell you.

And what Ankit does not know will not hurt him. That was what I initially said to myself, but even to me, it sounded mean. I could never betray him like that.

And so, I started thinking of ways to justify what I was about to do. And since I was this desperate to meet Ronit, ideas started flowing almost immediately. I stopped at the most convincing one—I am doing this to get Ronit out of my system.

Though I knew something like that was not likely to happen. See—if I meet him, I can either fall out of love or fall in love with him. And meeting him for just five minutes gave me a pretty good idea as to which way I was more inclined to.

But I have no better excuse to justify what I am about to do.

And as I enter Shiro this evening, I realize exactly how big a mess I am getting myself into. For a moment, I think of running away, but the curiosity . . . I just have to meet him.

I look around the club but cannot spot him anywhere. I choose a stool near the bar and take a seat, waiting. Maybe I should've worn a dress. Almost everyone here is wearing one. But when I had been deciding on what to wear, I somehow just could not bring myself to choose a dress. That would officially be dressing up. And then this would officially be a date. So I had chosen to wear denims instead.

Oh, okay. I probably shouldn't lie. I am wearing this really cool party wear top in deep violet, teamed with skinny black jeans. The top almost reaches my mid-thighs and looks pretty much like a dress and the jeans looks pretty much like stockings. So even though I am not wearing a real dress, I am quite close to being 'dressed up'. But they are two widely different things, aren't they? I am not officially dressed up.

I see him enter the club and look around. His eyes stop at me and I give him a short wave.

'Hi Vatsala,' he greets me with a kiss on my cheek. It burns a hole there. I swear.

'Hey,' I make my facial muscles move to give an appearance of a smile.

'You look nice,' he looks at me and says.

'Er, thanks,' I reply. Even though I don't mind compliments, if you compliment me the first time you see me, I will think that either it is a formality, or you are hitting on me. And since the last time we met, we had five other people with us, I consider this the first time we are meeting.

'So? How are things going?'

'Nice. I am really enjoying my job at Metro,' I reply honestly.

'Really? I thought it must be kind of . . . boring? Unglamorous?'

'Yeah. We don't get the kind of mad fan following you have, but it's decent,' I smile. 'I mean, the attention we get at Metro is okay. We are not exactly celebrities like you, it being a news channel, but still, it is fun.'

'Come to MTV. Then you will know what the real fun is,' he laughs.

'That was the plan, initially. But I never knew where to start. Never cared enough to find out,' I shrug.

'Hmm . . . as long as you are happy with what you are doing, it's all cool,' he smiles.

We stay silent for a while, not knowing what to say. I read it in an article somewhere that weather is one of the most commonly used topics people use to make conversation. I think about bringing that up. But, no. It would sound so—

'So, do you like it here at Mumbai?' Ronit asks, putting my thought process to an end.

'Yeah, it's nice. The weather is pretty harsh though.'

'It has always been. Born and bred here, I am used to it.'

'For me, it was a drastic change. I'd never faced such extreme climate,' I say.

'Where are you from?'

'Ranchi.' I thought he knew that. After all, he asked me if I like Mumbai or not. So he must have known I was not from here.

'Nice.'

We run out of topic once again. I have no idea how, after all those million chats on Facebook, we do not have anything to talk about.

Eventually, I say, 'I was surprised that you remembered me that day at the shoot.'

'Yeah, that day when I looked at you, I did recognize you. But I wasn't sure.'

'Of course! With so many pretty faces in your friend list.'

'C'mon! You always stood out. You were the most . . . interesting of the lot,' he says.

'Interesting? In a good way or is this just a polite way of telling me that I am weird.'

'Definitely in a good way,' he grins. Ooh, that dimple! I am falling in love again.

'Oh. I never thought you even knew me!'

'How could I not? We've chatted so many times.'

'Yes, but I never thought you remembered. I never thought you even realized I was the same girl you talked to the previous day,' I say.

'What? My memory isn't that bad!' he laughs. 'You can test me if you want!'

'Okay. When was the first time you noticed me?'

'Your first message on Facebook. I did not have that big a fan following. It was not difficult to differentiate people.'

'When is my birthday?' I ask next.

'Umm . . .'

'Do I have a boyfriend?'

'No,' he says. I do not correct him. Yes, I did not have a boyfriend when I was Facebook-stalking Ronit. But now I do. But it is not necessary for Ronit to know yet.

'Which conversation do you remember the best?'

'When I sent you the link to that photo of me on the beach.'

'The semi-stripped photo,' I say, remembering how I had fallen for him even worse after seeing that picture of him.

And from here, the conversation gets easier, and interesting. We talk about all kinds of things in the world, laughing all the while. I had forgotten how much I used to enjoy my conversations with him. Looks were not the only reason why I had fallen for him. In fact, looks had stopped playing a role after a while. It was the things he said. He always said good, witty things. He always made me laugh.

And as I now realize how much I had been missing all that, I feel a tinge of regret. Did I choose too early? Did I make a mistake by letting him go?

'Oh, darn,' he says and I smile. *He said 'darn'. He still uses that word.* 'It has been three hours! Where did time fly?'

'I didn't realize it either,' *I say honestly.*

'I had to be somewhere. I'm already late by fifteen minutes.'

'Then go!'

'I don't want to,' *he meets my eyes and says seriously.*

A shiver runs up my spine. This is not happening for real. This is not happening for real. My brain refuses to accept that Ronit Oberoi is actually showing interest in me. This is simply unreal.

'I don't know why I didn't notice you before,' *he wonders aloud.*

'Because it was Facebook. The virtual world. It is stupid to have a relationship with someone at a social networking site. Someone you have never even met,' *I say, faking a serious expression on my face.*

'True,' *he laughed.* 'Never mind! I found you now.'

I smile back. And do not tell him I have a boyfriend.

And before I know, he moves forward and kisses me on the lips. I freak out a little at first, and then realize that it was just a goodbye peck 'See you,' *he says and turns to leave.*

But he does not leave. Instead, he turns back around and pulls me closer to himself. He holds me by my waist and presses my body against his. And then, his lips come down on mine. He kisses me with no mercy. There is no subtleness, no tenderness. No one can look at us and say that this is our first kiss.

His lips grind against mine and his tongue raids my mouth. It explores every inch of it, ruthlessly. Meanwhile, I can feel his hand slowly making its way downwards, from where it had been resting on my waist. He pulls me even closer and increases the force of his mouth on mine even more. He is such a savage. And I like it. He is one of those men, who can make a girl get her climax just by one kiss. And I think I am pretty close to it.

At long last, he breaks the kiss and moves back to look at my face. His eyes never leave mine. There is a hint of a smile on his face, as if to say that he knows exactly what he has done to me.

We stare at each other wordlessly, before his face splits into an evil-ish smirk and he winks at me. And then, he turns around and leaves.

I stand here for ten whole minutes, reeling from the impact of what has happened. I met Ronit. I have finally met Ronit Oberoi. And we talked, and he said he had known me since my first message to him. This was kind of embarrassing. Because whenever I used to send random messages to him, I assumed that he did not even read them, let alone remember. Now I know. He did, and he did it quite well.

And he told me all about it. And we discussed everything that has ever happened between us in detail. Embarrassing details. Although he looked at my fan mails very fondly, to me they felt stupid. Imagine Brad Pitt actually reading a fan mail you sent him telling how much you loved the non-existent role he played in True Romance *and how you still remember the exact dialogues he had delivered in the movie. Exactly.*

But even though I felt mortified at the thought of him remembering my messages, he seemed quite pleased that I was such a big fan of his! But of course, all this is just at the back of my mind. What rules my mind at this minute is, undoubtedly, the kiss. The heavenly kiss.

I had never imagined it would get to this. And even though I had imagined several times, what it would be like if and when we kissed, nothing matched up to what it actually was like. Not even close.

I stand here, dumbfounded, still feeling his mouth on mine. The savage force, the persistent tongue, the intoxicating taste. I can still feel

his hand on my waist, slowly making its way downwards. I walk out
of the club and hail a taxi, remembering how nice I had felt when we
had first started chatting a year ago. This had felt even better.

I smile as I get into the cab. The thought of Ankit does not cross
my mind even once.

We'll Be Alright!

'Didn't I just *tell* you, babes? That we will kick Valli's ass?' Naitik said smugly.

'Of course! You are a genius,' I grinned. 'But what did you do? And how did you do it?' I asked. Naitik had called me as soon as I had got back and told me about this big offer from L'Oreal. They wanted to hire me, and they wanted to keep me. It was a one year long contract, which was as permanent as it gets. Obviously, we were thrilled.

But Naitik seemed even more thrilled than me. And smug. And cocky. Not that he was not like that always, but that day, it was even more than ever. And he was not telling me how he pulled it off. Considering the magnitude of influence Valli had on the people in the industry, I was not just surprised, but *shocked* to receive that offer from L'Oreal.

There was a reason everyone trusted Naitik so totally and completely. He not only pulled me off such a shitty situation, he even got me an offer this huge. And no one had any idea how. He must be some kind of a magician.

'Ah! You don't have to worry about that. That is taken care of. You just get all set to—'

'But I want to know! I'm curious,' I insisted.

'If I tell you, I will have to kill you, babes,' he said in a mock-serious tone.

'Kill me, then. But after telling me,' I laughed.

'No way! How can I kill my favourite client?'

'I'm your favourite? We only just started working together,' I was genuinely surprised.

'So what? I have already had more fun with you in this short time than I have had with clients I have been working with since years.'

'Really? How?'

'Valli,' he said.

'Argh. You are never going to tell me how you did it, are you?' I looked at him hopefully.

'Let's just say . . . I know how to uncover skeletons from people's pasts.'

'But you said Valli was clean!'

'That was *before*. Before *I* searched him. I know how to dig deep,' he said, in that super-arrogant tone of his.

'I can see that,' I smiled.

'So, forget about *what* and *how* and concentrate on pulling your act together. Attack parlours. You need to look ravishing. You start the shoot right after you sign. I have got all the documents ready,' he said and pulled out a thick wad of paper from his desk.

'I have to read all that?' I asked, with a look of horror on my face. If there is one thing I have absolutely zero appetite for, it is anything and everything legal. Unless it is a compulsion, I never read my contracts. But it has almost always been a compulsion, as I had no one else to do it for me. Until now.

'Unless you trust me—yes. I have read it, it is solid.'

'I trust you. Totally,' I said as I stood up to leave.

~

'What are you so happy about?' Vatsala asked me, as she roamed around the room, singing along with Eminem blasting from the speakers.

'What are *you* so happy about?' I shot back.

'I asked first,' she cocked her head back.

'I got an offer.'

'A *big* one?'

'Guess . . .' I said.

'A big one!'

'L'Oreal.'

'Are you kidding me?' Vatsala asked, with an expression of utter disbelief on her face.

'What? You think I cannot land L'Oreal?' I said in a fake-hurt tone.

'Shut up! Of course you *can*. But *did* you?'

'Yes!'

'Oh, awesome. I can just imagine your face all over magazines,' she let out. 'You just *have* to treat me for this. You just *have* to.'

'Sure! Anytime,' I smiled at her excitement.

'Not in a disc, though. In a restaurant. *Real* restaurant,' she said seriously.

'There are fake ones too?'

'Yeah, the ones in which people dance too. I want to go to one where people just *eat*. Such restaurants usually have better food too.'

'Okay, sure. Whatever you wish, whenever you wish,' I said. It was no fun going to dance clubs with Vatsala, anyway. She would just sit there, alone in a corner, humming along with the songs playing. She would not drink or dance. Not even watch people drink or dance. And the loud music did not allow us to talk either.

'Let's do this tonight! Tushar is not in town and Ankit is busy with his project or something. So we will get bored at home anyway,' she reasoned.

'You are making it sound like our boyfriends are our only ways of entertainment.'

'Not *only*, but *best*,' she winked. 'Anyway, let's go. I will go in jeans. Are you going to dress up?'

'No. I am wearing jeans too,' I said.

'Why?' she peeped out of the room and asked.

'No boys with us. Why waste time? We can relax,' I shrugged.

'So you are saying you dress up just to impress boys?' she raised one of her eyebrows at me.

'Boys, plural—when I am single. Boy, singular—when I am seeing someone.'

'And since your *boy* is not here, you will not wear a dress even when you are going out with me?'

'Exactly. What is the whole point of going through the pains of dressing up when there is no-one to see me?' As I said this, I suddenly started to miss Tushar. I wanted him there, with me. I would have dressed up all my life for him.

'But this is our first date, just you and me. You won't dress up for me?'

'*Uff!* You and your lesbian talk again,' I shook my head.

'So, you mean you have never considered *us*? That you do not find me attractive?' she asked, making a pose to flaunt her figure. Man, was I jealous!

'Actually, now that I think of it . . . we can work out some arrangement. In fact, I think we *should.*'

'You do?'

'Definitely. With Ankit so busy with his college and Tushar away most of the time . . .' I said.

'Now you're talking,' she rubbed her palms together and said.

'It is such a waste, with us living under the same roof,' I said and took a step towards her.

'Chhavi . . .'

'No one has to know . . .'

'Stop!' she said, taking a step backwards as I kept going towards her.

'What, baby?' I put on my best seductive face and asked.

'You are scaring me now,' she said, with a look of sheer horror on her face.

'Oh, don't be scared. It will be fun.' I made a move to touch her hand. She moved away. 'Trust me,' I added as an afterthought.

'I am out of here.'

'What? Why? What a waste it would be if, with such a chance in our hands, we don't *pleasure* each other—'

I was cut off by the sound of her door slamming. That was the last time she joked about *us*. And she never referred to the treat again. I don't think she ever trusted me enough to go out with me, alone, on a *date*.

~

'I really cannot come,' I said on the phone.

'I know. It's okay, I understand,' Tushar assured.

'I'm *so* sorry.' I felt so bad, Tushar had come to Mumbai and I could not meet him. Although it had been just a week since I had returned from Bengaluru, I had been missing him terribly and would have given anything to skip the shoot and be with him instead. But I could not bring myself to do that either. Not just because it was the biggest contract of my career, but also because Naitik had worked so hard (doing God knows what) to get me on that project. It would have been really selfish of me to pass on such a project. And immensely unfair to Naitik and my career.

So, I chose to stay. And as a result, I could not meet Tushar. He had not come for a long time. He had two hours' time after a full day of shoot. But even that was better than not meeting at all. We had learnt to be together in instalments.

Only, this time, I could not get time off to meet him. And I regretted it with all my heart. I felt like killing someone. I looked around. Why couldn't some photographer here die? Or maybe some model could come out of the green room, shouting about how the producer tried to get all cosy with her. Or how he smacked her butt every time he passed her by. Anything to cancel the shooting for the night.

All the time I had spent on the set that day, I had had my ears pinned for any indication of 'pack up' but it didn't come. And then I overheard someone say that it would take at least four more hours to wrap things up. And so, I had called Tushar to inform.

His understanding reaction only added to my guilt.

'It really is okay. Happens,' he said.

'I feel so bad about this. I wish I could run away and come to see you.'

'Don't. This is important for you and your career. Relax. We will meet sometime soon. I wanted to come to your set to meet you, but it will take too much time. I have a flight to catch,' he said regretfully.

'Yeah. And it will be a waste of time. Half of the time will be spent in getting here and getting back.'

'Exactly. So, we can't help the situation. So why worry about it? Chill. Next time.'

'When will the next time be?' I asked in a low tone.

'I don't know, baby. Things have been so busy for me lately . . . and now you have this contract . . .'

'I hate this. Long distance relationship.'

'I am not very fond of it either,' Tushar said.

Things had been hard for us. Not *I'm-dying-in-a-minute* hard. But definitely *I'll-die-if-this-keeps-happening* hard. Staying miles away from the person you love brings with it so many hitches. First and obvious—you are staying miles away from him. So you miss him. And a lot. And then, you have to have absolute faith in him. Which, in my case was not an issue. Somehow, Tushar never struck me as someone who would cheat on his girlfriend. But trusting a guy, who is almost always surrounded by insanely pretty models, is a difficult task.

To add to all this, our tight schedules were causing us some serious resentment. We didn't even talk on phone anymore. The texts were getting less frequent and the mails were getting shorter. We had forgotten things like Facebook and Gtalk existed. Skype never worked, as we were never free at the same time.

Life was hell.

'Why did I have to fall in love with you?' I said meekly.

'Hey, no matter what happens, no matter how difficult things are, never curse our love. This is real,' Tushar said with an intensity that could mean only one thing—he had said the same thing to himself a lot of times. Which meant he had been cursing our love too. Which meant he had been missing me madly too. It felt good. The thought brought a smile to my face.

'I didn't mean that. It is just that . . . staying apart is so difficult. I will never resent our love.'

'Yeah, staying apart is difficult. But this is only temporary. We won't be this busy always.'

'Right. I might be unemployed soon,' I said.

'And that would be awesome! You can come and stay with me 24 × 7. We will both be nomads,' Tushar laughed.

'Yeah. That would be super-fun,' I joined in his laughter. It felt nice to share a laugh.

'See? It isn't that bad. We're doing just fine,' he said.

'But I won't be unemployed any time soon. This is a one year contract.'

'But you can always screw up! Then they will fire you! Do that! I am selfish.'

'That I can see. You want me to end my career for your ulterior motives,' I said.

'Yes! And if it doesn't happen, I will do something bad. Something that would totally ruin my reputation. Then I will not get any offers. So I will come settle in Mumbai. Get a regular job, maybe.'

'You don't have to ruin your reputation for that. You can just *not* take up any assignments.'

'I can do that but that way, it would be a lot more difficult for me. Once I get an amazing offer, I just can't bring myself to pass it, you see,' Tushar said.

'Point. So destroy your reputation then.'

'Get involved in some sex scandal and go to jail or something?'

'Nice! Not something very big, though. I don't think we would get a chance to romance properly in jail,' I said.

'Okay, so I will do something bad, but not *that* bad.'

'Exactly.'

We laughed together for a short moment before he said seriously, 'We will find a way, I am sure.'

I paused for ten seconds and replied, 'Yes, we will.'

A Sneak Peek

'Are you kidding me?' Vatsala asked, looking exasperated. 'How are you still be friends with that Allya? She hit on your guy! How can you not hate her?'

'What? I have forgiven her for that one incident. She is okay,' I shrugged.

'But she has the looks. She looks like *the other girl*. What if she steals Tushar from you?'

'Tushar loves me.'

'And that somehow solves everything?' Vatsala asked.

'Yes! And she is a really sweet person. Unless she is drunk, at least,' I said and we laughed.

'I will go clear the fridge of everything with alcohol in it, then,' she said and made a beeline to the kitchen.

I followed her, 'You never struck me as one of the jealous types.'

'I am not jealous. I am just concerned about you.'

'Don't be. She's no threat. I know how to handle my man! Not that my man needs much handling, though.'

157

'Your call. I was just looking out for you,' she shrugged.

'Why are you so . . .? I don't know what. You just seem a bit different. Something happened?'

'No. Nothing happ—'

'I will kill you if you lie again. Something happened, right? Ankit? Ronit?'

'I went out,' she said, and looked away from me. I looked at her, really pissed off. Neither of us had anything to say.

'So, after we decided that you will not, you still went out with Ronit. *Why*?' I asked.

'He asked me out.'

'And "no" didn't strike you as a reply?'

'I tried. But I really couldn't.' She said and paused. 'I love him, Chhavi. I really do! I love him. Even I had always thought it was a crush, but it wasn't. I love him and there is nothing that can change it.'

'Vatsala! Are you out of your mind? You *love* him? How many times have you even met him?'

'Forget it. You will never get it. And just so you know—he asked me out again. And I am going. I want to meet him.'

'What about Ankit? You don't love him anymore?' I asked.

'Of course I love him! When did I say I do not love Ankit?'

'So you mean you love them both, then? Who do you love more?'

'I don't know. They are different *kinds* of love. I cannot compare,' she said.

'But you *will* have to choose one, you know that? You can't have it all. And I am right here. Whenever you need me.'

'As if that would help things! You will just make me stay with Ankit. I know I am alone in this. But I will find a way . . .'

'There is more to the story, isn't it? You have that look on your face. What are you hiding, Vatsala?' I asked.

'He kissed me. And it was amazing. I would have told you

exactly how amazing but I don't think you would be interested in knowing. You would just prefer calling me a slut, wouldn't you?'

'I would never say such a thing! How can I ever even think of saying that to you?'

'No? Then you would probably give me another lecture on how I cannot have both of them at the same time. But you know what? It is not something I have control over. I love Ankit. And I love Ronit. And I cannot live without either of them,' she shouted and ran to her room, banging the door behind her.

I was stunned. *What the hell just happened?*

I still had no clue why Ronit was so important for her. And how someone in her right mind could even consider leaving someone like Ankit. But it was her life, her decision. And if she really loved Ronit the way she thought she did, who was I to interfere?

But I wanted to interfere. As a friend, I could not let her do what she was doing. To herself. To Ankit. And to Ronit. But I could not do anything to stop her either. She simply was not listening to anything I had to say.

~

'Hey,' I said as I let Allya in, a couple of hours later. Vatsala wasn't home. Purposefully. She still wasn't cool with the idea of forgiving Allya for what she had done at Tara's reception. And there was this other tiny reason—she was mad at me.

We didn't say anything as we took seats around the living room.

'You know how sorry I am for that night, don't you? I was not in my senses. I had been having a bad time at work . . . and that day was particularly bad. But that does not justify what I did. All I can say is—I am very sorry.'

'It's okay. I understand,' I said and smiled a little.

'And I really didn't know you guys were going out!'

'We weren't. Not till then. Then, we had an open relationship. Now, we are in a real relationship,' I explained.

'Oh. Open relationship? And then you fell in love, of course. And you started wanting more. Happens always,' she said matter-of-factly.

'Happened to us, for sure,' I replied.

'Great! You guys look cute together. So, where is he now? Does he stay in Mumbai?'

'He stays nowhere. Just goes to places for work.'

'He doesn't have a permanent address? A flat he rented somewhere? Nothing?' she asked.

'No, he is just too busy to maintain a residence,' I laughed at her reaction. I have found that when she is not fretting about her career or is not busy getting drunk, she is a really sweet person.

'So how do you guys see each other? Whenever he is in the city? For work?'

'Yeah. And he comes to visit when he has time. And I went to see him once.'

'Hmm . . . but long distance? Must be difficult?' she asked.

'Yeah, it's difficult. I want to spend more time with him and all. But truth is, even if we were in the same city, we won't meet much more than we do now. Things are really busy at work . . .'

'Still, long distance is a completely different thing . . . . Aren't you worried? About what will happen next?'

'We will see when it comes to it,' I said.

'You will stay that casual about everything? What about the future?'

'I haven't thought about the future much . . . things are going okay at present. I am happy.'

'And that's what matters,' she smiled.

I smiled back.

Long after she had left, the thought still bugged me. Why did everyone have to raise eyebrows or worry whenever I told them that I was in a long distance relationship? We were just two regular people who were in love with each other and could not live in the same city at the moment.

The moment. That was the main concern. No one knew how long that moment was. *What if five years from now, we are still at the same place we are at now? What if we never are in the same city? What if he is always busy, always a nomad? Will we never grow in this relationship? Was this all there was to it? Will we never have a place together? Will we not have a more stable relationship? Will we never . . . have a family?*

As I sat alone, brooding about this, I got a text from him:

Tushar: There?
Chhavi: Yeah!
Tushar: Busy?
Chhavi: No . . .
Tushar: Skype!

'Hi,' I smiled as his face appeared on the screen. 'I have missed you.'

'Same here. Been such a long time since we last met. But never mind. Soon.'

'How soon?' I asked, hopefully.

'I don't know yet,' he looked unsure. 'There was that contract I told you about . . . for which I was coming to Mumbai this week. But I don't think I can, now.'

'Why?' I asked, as I felt a little sad inside. I was careful not to let it show in my expression.

'There is this assignment in Malaysia, which can do wonders to my career. If I can get it, I can overcome all the . . .' he stopped himself from saying the rest.

But I knew what he was talking about. All the postponed

meetings and cancelled contracts had not been reflecting very well on him. And his image had not been the same since. He needed a major career move to give him the boost he needed to get him back on track. And the Malaysia assignment could be just that.

'I know. So, you are taking that up?' I asked.

'I want to, if I am offered. They have short-listed four photographers. I am one of them . . .'

'You will get it, I'm sure,' I acted like the perfect supportive girlfriend. I had no other choice.

'What are you doing?' Vatsala asked, as she peeped into my room. She was not mad at me anymore. She was just a kid. She did not know how to stay mad for long.

'Chatting with Tushar,' I said.

'Video chatting, right? So why are your shirt buttons closed?' she asked.

'What?'

'What? Isn't that what people in long distance relationships do when they chat on Skype?'

I stared at her in disbelief and said nothing.

'Why are you looking at me like that? What is the purpose of video-chatting otherwise? Just to see each other's face? That is like—*so cheesy*,' she continued.

I stayed silent.

'Hi Vatsala,' Tushar said after a while.

'Hi—oh damn! He can hear me? Oh God, Chhavi! Tell me he can't! Can he?' she let out.

I nodded, as Tushar said, 'I can. Every word.'

She stared at me in horror and ran away, shutting the door behind her.

We laughed. 'This girl,' I said as I shook my head, smiling.

'She did have a point, though. What a waste it will be if I don't get even a peek . . .' Tushar said.

'Very clever.'

'Is it working?' he asked, looking hopeful.

'I don't think so,' I thrust out my lower lip.

'But I have missed you . . . Like, a lot. So, am I getting any?'

'Am I?'

'What do you want?' he asked.

'Exactly what you want. A peek. Of . . .'

'You have such a dirty mind!'

'What? I didn't even say anything. You are the one who assumed it to be . . . whatever you assumed it to be!' I said.

'But you were implying that. I could read your mind!'

'Not are not very good at it, clearly.'

'Oh yeah? What *did* you mean then?' he asked.

'Forget it! I don't want it anymore . . . Too many details. I lost interest.'

'I think I can revoke it.'

'I would like to see you try,' I said.

We went on like that all night. Well, not *exactly* like that, but our conversation was equally, if not more, awesome that full night. We talked and talked and talked. It had been such a long time since we had had a real conversation, we had needed this. That night was one of the best nights of my life.

And that was when we did not ultimately remove—or even unbutton, for that matter—any article of our clothing.

Being Selfish

'Chhavi!' Vatsala called from the living room.

'What?' I said in a muffled tone, my head still dug into my pillow. What was wrong with her? Why did she have to take to waking up so early recently? Oh, yes. Gym.

She had suddenly decided that she just *had to* start going to the gym. I asked her why, as she already had the perfect figure without having to work for it and she looked at me as if I was an alien. *Figure* is not the only thing people join gyms for. What about *health*? Wasn't that the most important of all? I had no answer to that. All the people I know went to gym for their physique. Health might just be taken as an added advantage!

'Come here!' she shouted. 'Fast! Just come. You just have to see this!' She sounded so excited, I was sure she had seen Brad Pitt for real.

'Shut up. Let me sleep,' I said and turned on my side.

'It is about Tushar! He is on the news.'

The next moment, I was in the living room, with my eyes transfixed by the television. Tushar's photograph was put in an inset in the left corner of the screen and the newsreader talked about his latest accomplishment—*the Malaysia contract*. He got it! As the reader went on about his history, talking about how he had started and where he was now, I felt proud of him.

I listened to the newsreader talk about all the big things Tushar Mehra had achieved and I could not help but smile foolishly. I would have given him an awesome *private party* if he was there then, if you know what I mean.

Anyway, so when she moved to the next slot of the news, I picked up my phone to call Tushar.

'Hi Tushar! I heard it on the TV. I am *so* happy for you. Congratulations!'

'Thanks. I was about to call you. I got to know about it yesterday.'

'Yesterday? So why didn't you tell me? This is big news!' It felt like I was more excited about the deal than him.

'I was going to,' he said shortly.

'Is something wrong? What is it?' I asked. It was odd. Tushar not telling me about what was probably the biggest deal of his career. It kind of hurt.

'We need to talk. And not like this. In person. We need to meet.' He sounded so serious, I was almost absolutely sure he was going to talk about breaking up.

'Are you planning to leave me?' I blurted out.

'What? No! I am not planning to leave you. Why would you even think such a thing?'

'I don't know. You just . . . sound so . . . grave.' Yes, that was the word. That was how he sounded. Grave.

'No, baby. I am not going to break up with you. In fact, I was thinking . . .'

'What?' I held my breath. What can be so serious an issue? I had never seen Tushar like that. I knew something must be worrying him. *Really* worrying him.

'I hate to do this over phone. I will come to you as soon as possible. And then we will talk?'

'Should I be worried?' I have no idea why I asked that. Wasn't I already worried?

'Not at all,' he assured.

'Okay, then I will wait.'

'I'll try to come whenever possible.'

'Soon?' I asked.

'Very soon.'

~

That entire week, I was a mess. I had no idea what Tushar wanted to talk about, but I had never seen him that stressed out. Between the two of us, I usually was the one fretting about stupid things and he was the calm one, laughing at me because I worried so much. So this was new. And this was scary.

I wanted him to come to Mumbai as soon as possible and tell me what it was all about. Hell, I did not mind doing it over phone, even. But he was adamant. Face to face was what he wanted. And somehow, neither of us had time to visit the other for a full week. I was dying. I just had to know what it was all about. So, as soon as I got to know that I had a day off, I went to see him. He was at Pune then, so it was not a problem for me. He knew I was coming. And he was there to receive me at the airport.

When I saw him, I am sure the smile on my face was the broadest I had ever smiled. Just looking at him relaxed my nerves. He stood there, tall and handsome, with the twinkle in his eyes and that adorable stubble, smiling at me. I felt a rush of affection towards him. Sometimes, when I saw him, I felt like shouting and telling the world *he's mine!*

It was like—when I did not see him for weeks at an end, I forgot how good he looked. I usually dismissed it as, *Naah!*

He can't be that good. I convinced myself that I was probably exaggerating his good looks in my mind. So by the time I saw him again, I underestimated his looks so much that it amazed me to find him so handsome. Happened every time.

He came forward to hug me and I surrendered to the hug. It felt so good to be in his arms, after so long. When you commit to someone, after a while, you realize that the *physical* part of your relationship does not only mean the *sexual* part. Yes, in the beginning, the sex overpowers everything else. But once you really start loving someone, the small touches, the pecks on the cheeks and the hugs matter equally. Especially when you do not get them regularly.

And I was *very* deprived. *I was fed up of loving him in instalments.*

I wanted a real relationship.

That day, when we reached his hotel room, we, for once, did not start ripping each other's clothes off. We knew we had very little time, only a few hours together, but making love somehow was not what we craved. Our ground rule went into the bin.

It was company. We craved each other's company. We wanted to be with each other, look at each other and talk.

Talk.

We made small talk for a while. And it killed me. How did things get so awkward between us? When did we get so aloof, so detached? We were discussing the weather, for God's sake! Tears prickled my eyes. Two more minutes of that and I would have started crying.

I had to get to the point. I had to get it over and done with. We needed to talk about whatever it was that had been bothering him, and get it out of our systems. I could not wait anymore.

'Tushar . . .' was all I had to say. The look on my face must have given my message to him loud and clear. His expression changed.

'Yes. Uh, okay. Where do I begin? See, this Malaysia project

. . . it is very nice and it would be really great for my career if I take it, but I think I am going to pass it on . . .' he started.

'Why?' I was surprised. Is this what he wanted to talk about? Career? Is that why he wasn't excited when I'd called to congratulate him for getting the deal?

'Because . . . *this*. Us. You see how . . . how distant we have become? We meet once or twice a month, for a few hours together. And we don't even have time to talk to each other. Not even on phone. If I take this offer . . .'

I stared at him, and said nothing.

'. . . I fear our relationship will suffer very badly,' he said.

'But why *this* deal? Can't you just take this deal and pass along the next, less important one, maybe? This deal is important, isn't it?'

'It is. But even if I don't take it, it won't harm me.'

'It would. I know all about it, Tushar. You can't fool me,' I said. I knew how big that deal was. And I knew how many other photographers had been working terribly hard to get it. And I knew how hard Tushar had worked hard to get it. And when he had it, it really did not make sense to let it pass. 'Tushar, this is the biggest opportunity of your life! Why—'

'I don't care! More offers will come,' he said.

'Yes, they will. Many more such, and even bigger offers will come. But that is in the *future*! You have this *now*. Take it.'

He stayed silent for a while. I was getting nervous again. There was more to the story. It can't be just that he didn't want to take this deal because we were growing apart. Because we'd been growing apart since a long time and how will not taking up this one deal change anything? There was something more. Something to do with the contract . . .

'What is it, Tushar? I know you are keeping something from me. Tell me,' I went to him and asked.

He looked at me and held my hand. 'It requires me to go to Malaysia. For two months. Last week of October.'

I didn't say anything. I *couldn't* say anything. Last week of October was *just three days away*. Ever since we had started dating, we had met only a handful of times. When we were in an open relationship, it had been easier. Not only because we did not need each other as much, but also because we actually saw each other a lot more than we did after we had started dating. It was just a coincidence that his work didn't need him to come to Mumbai that often anymore. And my career had taken a hike, so I was almost always short on time too. And it was taking its toll; our relationship was suffering.

We barely ever met. We barely ever talked on phone. We left each other random *miss you* messages on the phone. And mails had long before ceased to exist. No. What we had now wasn't a relationship.

I felt like crying.

'I'm not going,' he said softly, studying my expression intently.

I knew I should act like a good girlfriend, like a good person, and ask him to go. I knew I should not ask him to stay just for me. Not at the expense of his career. But I could not let him go. Call me selfish, and that is what I was, but I simply could not afford to lose him.

I tightened my grip on his hand.

'Chhavi . . . Baby, I'm not going.'

Our relationship was hanging by a thread. Yes, we both loved each other. But we did not have any control over our schedules. If we wanted our relationship to work, we needed to make sacrifices. And Tushar was starting to do exactly that. And I would do the same when needed.

But the question was—even if he passed that offer, he would have to take others. And so, instead of spending the whole two months in Malaysia, he would spend them travelling around India, and would be equally busy. We would probably meet once or twice in that time span. So what was the whole point of not taking up the Malaysia project just so we could meet a couple of times for a few hours? Were the visits worth it?

I did not like the answer to that last question. And I knew our relationship was doomed either way. If he went to Malaysia, it would die then and there. If he did not, it would die slowly, over the next few months.

'Go. This is important for you,' I said at long last.

'No way,' he shook his head. His face had that conviction, the one that says he would never let me go. I wanted to believe in it. I wanted to believe in him. But I was afraid to hope. 'Yes, this is important for me. But I can do without it,' he looked at me smiled.

'But it won't help! Even if you don't take this project, others will come. And you will be equally busy. And we will be equally apart. So—'

'We won't—'

'How? We've been saying we'll try and make this work. But this is *not* working. This has no future now—' I said but he cut me off.

'Listen!' Tushar suddenly raised his voice and silenced mine. 'We *do* have a future. But we don't have it easy. We have to work for it. And I am willing to.'

'But Tushar . . . even if you let this project go, how will it help things?' I asked softly.

'I am thinking of something. I need to get a place. Since you live in Mumbai, I guess I would settle there. Makes sense . . .'

I was touched. He was taking this seriously. He was thinking about *us*, and he was making an actual effort to make it work with me. I had always known that it would be difficult for us to have a future together. To start with—because of what happened with his parents, he did not believe that relationships last. And then—he had never really been in love with a girl before. Not of the serious kind.

I had never expected him to fall that madly in love with me. I had thought that the ghosts from his past would not let him. I had never known that he would begin to care about me so much.

So when I saw him willing to give our relationship a chance, it was nothing short of a miracle. Half-heartedly, I said, 'But . . . you will still have to travel that much . . .'

'I am planning to take work slow from now. I don't need to work this hard. Even if I do half of what I have been doing, I will be fine.'

'No! Your career will suffer!' I said.

'Don't worry about that. I have been thinking. There are good possibilities in Mumbai too. If I start concentrating on projects that are Mumbai-based, I think I can still have pretty awesome chances.'

I let it all sink in. And then said, 'So, you want to get a place in Mumbai, so we could be closer and meet more regularly? And you are also planning to take your career slow so that our relationship can have the first priority?' I asked, almost breathless. It was too good to be true. I died and went to paradise.

'Exactly.'

'You know . . . I love you.'

Sacrifices That We Make

'He let it go?' Are you kidding me?' Vatsala asked, all big-eyed. She still did not believe what we were doing.

'No, I am serious,' I laughed. 'He really is passing that offer and re-locating to Mumbai, so we can be closer. And we can meet more. He's doing this for us.' Just the thought of it brought a smile to my face.

'And you're letting him? He is doing this and you are actually cool with that?'

'What?' I don't think we were on the same page. She was actually *angry* that he was shifting to Mumbai. I looked at Ankit for support, but he shrugged in a I-have-no-idea-what-got-into-her kind of way.

'You are letting him kill his career and come to Mumbai? Just so you can have a better relationship? It is really selfish of you.'

'He is not *killing* his career! And it is *not* selfish! I am going to put my career as a second priority from now on too,' I defended. I knew Vatsala didn't mean any harm, but it still hurt. I had thought that she would understand, and she would support me on that. Because, after all, she was the one always saying that we looked cute together. But she took to the news so badly that I started to suspect something was really wrong . . .

'But *why*? Why put career as a second priority?'

'Because our relationship is more important,' I stated the obvious.

She threw her hands up in the air, as if I was a spoilt teenager and she was fed up of trying to reason with me. 'Why are relationships so important?' she asked, more to herself and less to us.

I chose to stay silent. I knew it had nothing to do with Tushar and me. *Something was wrong between Vatsala and Ankit. And it had something to do with Ronit. And that kiss.*

'Maybe because relationships *mean* more?' Ankit asked.

'Well, I don't really get what you both are going on about. I don't see how,' she replied simply.

'Because, in the long run, that is what matters. Careers, money—they are all superficial. Surface. Relationships, people—they matter,' Ankit said.

'So that is why you have been paying so much attention to *our* relationship, all this while?' Vatsala asked.

'What does that mean?' Ankit asked.

'You know exactly what that means. Since almost a month now, you have barely even been here. In the same city, but never free to meet.'

'Vatsala, I had my project to complete. I *did not* meet you more often because I *could not* meet you more often!'

'So, that is not putting your career before me?' Vatsala asked.

'It was just temporary. I had a deadline.'

'That is what you always say!'

'Because that is what happens! I am at college, I'm a student. What else do you expect?' Ankit asked.

'I expect you to think about me a little too.'

'I do think of you. I have been calling you—'

'Just calling every now and then does *not* mean you are committed to our relationship,' Vatsala said.

'I am trying, Vatsala! But I have studies to take care of too. I thought you understood.'

'I did. But I am fed up. We are in the same city and we meet once in ten days!'

'Okay, so now I am here. And you will be my first priority always, I promise.'

'What if it is too late? What if I don't want this anymore? What if I don't want—You. Me. Us.'

Ankit opened his mouth to say something, but could not seem to find words to relay what he was thinking. He looked at me, and I shook my head helplessly.

I had no idea what Vatsala was getting all filmy about, but I did suspect that it had something to do with Ronit. Whenever she was in one of her moods, it *always* had to do with Ronit.

'I, uh, I should probably leave you guys alone—'

'No! You're not going anywhere. Stay right there,' she suddenly shouted. 'And just listen to me. I don't want to hear anything from you. You've told me everything and you've told me enough. I think I can judge the situation pretty well depending upon that.'

'I don't think you should interfere—' Ankit tried to come to my rescue but she cut him off too.

'*You stay out of this.* Let me deal with Chhavi first and then we will talk about *us*,' she looked at him and said pointedly. Then, she turned to me and said, 'Listen Chhavi, you are destroying him, yourself and both your careers. Especially his, as of now. If you let him pass such a fab offer and let him settle here in Mumbai, it would be a beginning to the end of your relationship with him. Don't do this.'

She paused for a minute and I asked slowly, barely daring to look at her, 'Why do you think his relocating to Mumbai will ruin everything?'

'Because he is not in the best frame of mind right now! He is taking this decision in haste. He misses you and he loves you too much to stay away from you, so he is giving up so much to come here. But what about later? What happens after your honeymoon phase ends? Don't you think he would resent you?'

'Not if his career goes well,' I said.

'Which it won't. Not unless he is insanely lucky and lands one of those permanent positions in one of those big firms around here. Like Mystique. Or Chrome. I know he might actually get them, but tell me—what are the odds?'

I didn't even want to think.

'See, Chhavi,' her tone softened. 'If you guys do this, a couple of years down the line, best case scenario—you still love each other and you both have average or extremely shitty careers, depending upon the degree to which you decide to compromise with it now. And worst case scenario—you both start regretting putting your careers in the back lane, and separate. Even if you don't break up, you silently start resenting each other for being the reason why your lives suck.'

'But we love each other,' I murmured. Wasn't that one fact supposed to solve everything?

'Yes you do. *Today*. What about tomorrow? The next week? The next month? Year? Are you *that* sure? Even if you *are* sure today, that you will love him forever, the truth is, *you don't know*. And even if we assume that you *do* love him this much all your life, what about him? Will he love you the way he does now once he sees his career going down because of you?'

I didn't know what to say. Seeing Vatsala like that shocked me. I was freaked out at seeing the change in her. She had a very clear picture of how to deal with my love life, but she could not see what she was doing to hers. And in my heart, I knew she was right and I was being selfish. But I could not let Tushar just go. What about our love?

'Nothing is forever,' I heard her say softly as I made my way to my room.

I needed to think.

~

About ten minutes later, I heard the front door bang. Moments later, there was a knock on my door.

'Come in,' I said, wiping my tears away. Vatsala would talk to me and we would find out a way to deal with the situation. It was not all over yet.

'Are you okay?' I heard Ankit say and I looked up, amazed to find him standing there.

'Ankit . . . I thought it was Vatsala.'

'Vatsala left for—I don't know where. She just banged the door and left.'

'Oh. You had a bad fight?' I asked.

'Kind of. I just did not know what we were fighting about.'

I gave a short laugh. 'She was in a flow. God knows what got into her.'

'Exactly. She said something like it would be my fault if she had cheated on me sometime the last month, because I was this busy and never had time for her,' he said.

'Oh.' So this was what it was all about? She was feeling guilty about that kiss with Ronit and was finding a way to transfer the blame?

'Do you know what that was all about?' Ankit asked, studying my face.

'I have no clue,' I lied.

He nodded, thinking about something. 'I think this time it's serious. It's not just one of her moods . . . I think something is up. Something major.'

I looked away, fearing my expression would give away what I was thinking.

He looked at me. 'Anyway, about what she said to you . . . I think, to a certain extent, I agree with her. You guys are rushing into this. You probably should not be this rash.'

I had been expecting him to ask me not to take it too seriously, as she didn't mean what she said, that she did not know what she was talking about. But that did not happen.

'You think this is a mistake?' I met his eye and asked. 'But we do have to start *working* on our relationship to make it work.'

'I know. But this . . . this is too big a compromise to start with. This is a big project and he needs it at the moment. I know he says that he does not care, but he is lying. You know how hard he has worked for this. How can he not want it? If he passes this, he *might* end up resenting you.'

I stayed silent for a while. I knew what he was saying was the truth. And I knew what else it meant. 'We are *over*,' I said, sadly.

'No, you're not,' Ankit laughed. 'You can make it. You just have to try. You will just have to deal with it for a couple more months, till when his contract is over. Then try compromising with your respective careers and balancing your personal and professional lives. If you are meant to be, you will make it,' he said simply.

'The way you put it . . . it actually feels kind of easy.' I felt relieved almost instantly. *I will still have Tushar. Yay!*

'It isn't really easy, but workable, I am sure,' he smiled.

'Thank you so much. You're a genius.'

'*Naah*,' he shrugged. 'I should probably get going. I have to find her.'

'Go!' I said.

'I just hope she has cooled down a little by now. That girl scares me.' Although he said that in good humour, he did look kind of scared.

I just wished Vatsala would make up her mind quickly. I hated to see her and Ankit in such states.

Chances That We Take

When I thought about it, I decided that it made perfect sense. If I let Tushar go for that contract, I would not necessarily lose him. I would just have to make some additional effort to take care that things between us ran smoothly. And he would have this dream project. Was not that what was important at the moment?

And as Ankit said—*if we were meant to be, we would make it*. That decided, all I had to do was make Tushar understand the same. And I found the perfect time. He had come to Mumbai and we were in my apartment. Since he was in the city just for the night, it did not make sense for him to stay in a hotel. And I had insisted that he came to my place. I had things on mind that could not wait. I had to take care of stuff.

As he did something on his BlackBerry, I slowly crawled up to him and rested my head on his shoulder. He put his one arm around me and held me close, but still did not look up from his phone, though. I looked up and pulled his face by the chin to make him look at me.

'What are you doing?' I asked.

'Just checking my mails.'

'And now seemed to be the perfect time?'

'You had something better in mind?' he raised an eyebrow. That made him look immensely sexy. I wanted to eat him. *Later*, I told myself. We had more important things to discuss before.

'Actually, I do,' I said.

'And that is . . .?'

I sat up straight and turned to face him directly. I took a deep breath, ready to start. Then, at the last moment, I was hit by a stroke of genius and decided to kiss him first. That would get him into a much better mood. I moved closer and kissed him softly on the lips, followed by his nose and forehead. Several kisses later, when he looked happy enough, I decided it was time.

'I think you should consider taking up the Malaysia project,' I said softly.

'Didn't we already decide what we are going to do?' his smiled vanished in a fraction of a second.

'Yes, we did. But it was stupid! We don't need to do that. We can make this work even if you take this project. You don't need to pass this.' I took a breath. 'See, it doesn't really matter if you shift here *after* this Malaysia thing is done, does it?'

He didn't say anything.

'So what we can do is—carry on like we've been doing all this while, and when you come back, we can go on as we'd planned. It's just a matter of two months,' I said.

'I don't know about you, but I am not sure I can handle another two months like this.'

'Aww. That's so sweet of you,' I grinned.

'Chhavi, I am serious,' he said, and his tone said the same.

'I . . . Tushar . . . it's just two more months . . .'

'. . . after which something else would come up. Something equally, or even more amazing. And then we would think we can go as per our plan *after* that. But it will keep on happening again and again. And I am not taking that risk. We are going to go as planned. I don't know why you were even thinking about it after we had already come to a decision. I am going to refuse to take that offer, it's high time. They would need to contact the substitute soon.'

'I can't let you do this . . .' I said, but it came out lower than I had expected.

'We have already discussed this. We cannot go on like this anymore, Chhavi. I am tired of missing you.'

'I miss you too. But this is important for you. I can't let you do this. Not for me,' I said.

'Then you will have to leave me.'

'*What?*' I felt like a steel knife was being stuck in my throat. It felt strangely constricted and tears filled my eyes instantly.

'You heard it right.'

'You want us to break up?' I could not believe he said that. Break up was something I never thought would happen to me. Not with Tushar. The guy always had the look of *permanent* about him.

'I don't *want* us to break up. But I think we should. Given the choices that we have—I would prefer breaking up to carrying on like this.' His voice sounded so . . . *mechanical.*

'No, Tushar, we *cannot* break up,' I tried to make him understand. The tone of desperation would make him understand how important it was for me.

'And we *cannot* carry on like this either,' he stated simply.

'Are they my two options? Either to make you take up the offer and forget you forever or to let you give up that offer and see you resent me for a lifetime?'

'Yes. They are your only options. I would have loved to give you both, the Malaysia project and the relationship, but I cannot handle this anymore. I need to *decide.* And *soon.*'

'I can't let you stay. And I can't let you go,' I said, hoping he was kidding around.

'You can't have it both ways.'

We couldn't carry on like that anymore. That wasn't a real relationship. We were just living in denial, pretending that we even *had* a relationship. I was tired of missing him. I was tired of wishing we had more time together. I was tired of not being able to receive his calls, of not having time to reply to his mails. I was tired of him rejecting my calls and cancelling his trips because of work. I was tired of being together, and yet so away.

This had to end.

'Go,' was all I could say, as tears started flowing.

'What?'

'Tushar please . . .' I said between sobs. 'Just . . . go.'

At first, he looked like he wanted to protest. I could see his eyes shine with tears. I looked away. I could not bear to see him like this.

'You're sure about this?' he asked, as he got up from the bed and turned away.

'Hmm . . .'

He did not say anything at all. I sat there on the bed and watched him put on his clothes and my breath started to get more and more ragged. I tried to control myself, at least till he left. And I was pretty proud of the way I handled myself. I did not let my face show the extent to which I was hurting.

As he picked up his bag and walked out of the room, I silently got up from my bed and followed him into the living room. He reached the door and turned to me. And this time, along with the obvious pain, I could read other expressions in his face too. Hurt. Anger. Hatred. Disgust.

He looked at me with such *loathing* in his expression, that my heart almost stopped beating.

'You know . . . there was a reason I never believed in relationships,' he said. 'There was a reason why I never thought love matters. But then I met you . . . and everything changed. I *believed* in you, Chhavi. I thought this was real. And I thought we would last . . . but again, I was proved wrong.'

I wanted to tell him that it was not so. That what we had really was real. But I stay shut. I would say nothing to make him stay. *He had to go.*

'Thank you,' he said. 'For proving me wrong. For stopping me from giving up this project. It would have been such a stupid mistake,' he said, his voice getting louder with every word. 'I mean, *what was I thinking?* I was actually going to give that up? For what? *You?*' he laughed dryly.

I knew he was hurt. And I knew he was inflicting pain, just so he would feel better. What else could justify this behaviour? That he really did hate me? That he really was disgusted by me?

That can't be. *That just can't be.* That was one possibility I would never even consider being true. It hurt too much.

He turned the knob and pulled the door open. When he got out, he turned back and said, 'I really thought I loved you. I really thought that we were something. It's amazing how stupid I have been.'

And then he left. I wanted to say *I love you too.* I wanted to say that yes, we really were something. But instead, I stood there and watched him go.

It was like my world came to an end. What would I live for? My career? The glamour world? The families who send me marriage proposals? The people who watched me on screen and knew me as just a pretty face.

It was astounding how my life suddenly seemed so empty, without Tushar in it. Everything seemed shallow, as if I had nothing left worth living. I had imagined our whole future together. If I wanted a future, I wanted it only with Tushar. I could not imagine my life without him.

Long after he left, I still kept standing there, the tears flowing worse than ever. It was Vatsala who took me to my room, when she got back home from work. I think I would have stood there for an eternity otherwise. I had never seen Vatsala that distraught. Even when her own life was caught up in that big Ankit–Ronit mess, she still always seemed to have a certain strength about her. Not this time.

It felt like even though it was I who broke up, it was her life that was affected worse. We held each other and cried for a long time. I did not know who was comforting who. And I was kind of surprised to see Vatsala could even *do* all that—hugging and crying. She just never came across as a person capable of this. She had always projected herself as being so cold, that I had almost forgotten what she really was like.

'This is all my fault. I made you leave him,' she whispered.

I shook my head. 'No. It is no one's fault. We just weren't meant to be.'

'This is so . . .' she trailed off, shaking her head vigorously. 'I just never thought you guys would . . .'

'I never thought that too.'

'Won't you miss him?'

'All the time.'

'How are you going to live without him?'

I didn't reply to that. I had no idea.

Choices That We Make

Vatsala Tells Her Story—II

As I put on my dress this evening, I feel like shit. Chhavi and Tushar broke up yesterday, and it is somehow exceptionally hard on me. I knew that things were getting complicated between them, and it was I who told Chhavi that they should put their relationship in the back lane and make career their first priorities. But I never thought that it would happen. I had just never thought they would actually break up.

Now, when they are no longer together, I feel like I am the reason behind that. I had been looking for a justification for what I have been doing recently with Ankit and Ronit. I had been looking for a way to justify that relationships were not that important and weren't always meant to last. I was searching for a way to leave Ankit, and make it look like it wasn't something I did. It just wasn't meant to be. We weren't supposed to last.

And with that thought overpowering my ability to think coherently, I had forced my views on Chhavi. And she had seen a point in them. And now, all because of me, they have separated. So now, not only do I feel sad that they are not together anymore, I even feel guilty for

185

causing the break up. I have never seen Chhavi like that. She had barely slept all night, and she just kept staring at the wall. I wonder what must be going on in her mind.

How does it feel when you cut off a person from your life forever? Does everything change? How would I feel when I leave Ankit?

Yes, I have decided. I know I love Ankit a lot and would probably never get over him, but all I care for—at this moment—is Ronit. What I have been doing to Ankit was wrong anyway, and I feel immensely guilty about it. Even if I stay with him, a part of me would always be with Ronit. And that would be unfair to Ankit.

I love them both and I want to have them both. But it doesn't work that way, does it? I had to choose. And the choice had been killing me. But in the end, I have come to a decision—I cannot live not knowing what could be with Ronit. It is a big gamble. If I leave Ankit and go to Ronit, what are the odds that Ronit will fall for me one day? What are the odds that he will be as great as I think he is? There is no guarantee. But I don't care. I am willing to take the risk.

I love him enough.

'I'll be back soon,' *I say, entering Chhavi's room. I am relieved to see that she is not sitting on the floor anymore, like she had been doing since last night. And it feels nice to see that she has taken a shower and changed into fresh clothes. Maybe she should brush her hair too. Her hair is looking scary. Like horror-movie-ghost scary. I am about to pass her a comb when I stop myself. She broke up just yesterday. She should look it. If not downright devastated, then at least a little blue.*

'You'll be alright?' *I study her face. Maybe I should postpone my plans for tonight. She looks like she needs me.*

'Yeah. Allya is coming over.'

'Oh, nice. Take care then,' *I smile and turn to leave. I have forgiven Allya for what she had done long back. She has already had it so tough recently, so I have decided to spare her the guilt.*

'You are going to see Ronit, aren't you?' *she asks and I nod. She continues,* 'You're sure about this?'

'Yes, I am sure about this,' I reply.

'Choose wisely, Vatsala. Leaving someone you love hurts. I hope it all works out,' she smiles sadly.

'I hope so too,' I say and leave.

~

As I stand outside Club Escape, I feel strangely numb. I am going to do this. I am going to leave Ankit. Ankit, the guy who has always been by my side. Who has always loved me and cared for me, unconditionally. With whom I have spent the best parts of my life. Who has made me laugh and put a smile on my face whenever I have felt low. Who has always dealt with my drama happily. The only person in the world who actually understands me.

But if I stay with him and keep loving Ronit too, it would be wrong on my part.

And anyway, if I let Ronit go, I would always wonder how it could have been between us. And ultimately, I might start blaming Ankit for it all. I am that sort of a person. Irrational.

So Ankit has to go. For his own good.

I step into the club and make my way to the bar. We have decided to meet here. I do not look around to search for him because I know he is not here yet. I am early. As I sit here, waiting for him, I think about what I would say when he asks me for a drink. Should I tell him that I don't drink? Or do I order something and take a sip or two? The latter would be better, I decide. It might seem too prudish if I say I don't drink. And I want to make a good impression.

I look around me and see people bustling around the place. It is a busy night. Which is obvious, as it is a Saturday. Everyone is dressed impeccably. You cannot find a girl whose face isn't made up. Except me.

Oh God.

As I make my way to the washroom, I internally curse myself for being so stupid. I have come, with my face devoid of make-up, because

I thought it would make me look bad. Make-up always makes me look bad. I am one of those girls, who never look good made up. But this is Ronit. And I am meeting him, in a club. It is a date. I cannot go looking like this. He would think I don't care enough for him to go to the pains to apply a bit of colour on certain parts of my face.

I start with kohl and regret it instantly. I hadn't slept properly the last night, and the kohl only accentuates the dark shadows under my eyes. Damn. I'm really not someone who should apply make-up. I don't even know how to, anyway. As I try to rub a cotton bud to remove the kohl from my eyes, my phone buzzes. Ankit. I ignore it. I will call him. Later, when I get home.

I remove the eyeliner from my handbag and start applying it, when a thought crosses my mind—I would never have to dress up or apply make-up for Ankit. He likes me the way I am.

The thought makes me pause. Why am I leaving him? How can I leave him? It's Ankit. Ankit! I can't do this. I just can't . . . Not to him. Not to myself. I would die without him. My life is perfect. Uncomplicated. Why am I so adamant on destroying it? What will I do without him? I start panicking. I am still breathing hard when my phone rings again. Ankit! I am going back to him. I will tell him everything. He deserves the truth. And I am going to apologize. And I will hope that he forgives me.

'Ankit!' I exclaim into the phone, brushing away the tears that have suddenly made an appearance.

'Hello?' came a voice from the other end. It wasn't Ankit. I checked the display of my phone. Ronit.

'Hey, Ronit?'

'Hi, Vatsala. Are you there yet?' he asks.

'Yes, I am here.'

'Cool. I'll be there in five.'

'Great. I'll be at the bar,' I say and hang up.

What am I doing? In two minutes, I will be sitting at the bar, in a dance club, wearing a dress, with my face all made up, sipping a drink

I have never drunk before, chatting with a guy, sitting crossed-legged, maybe even flipping my hair from my face and throwing my head back and laughing as if he was the funniest person in the world. Like those heroines from the movies.

It is so not me.

But I can change. For Ronit. And I need to grow up anyway, right? I can't go on like this forever, I reason. Maybe I will take up smoking, even. It makes sense.

So I turn back to the mirror and put on the eyeliner. I am wearing all black, so I don't need that much coloured make-up anyway. Just some liner and mascara would do the trick. Though eyes have always been comparatively easier for me to deal with. Lips are what really bug me. I hate applying anything coloured on them. Sheer lip balms are almost as far as I would go. Even during my shoots, I barely even tolerate putting lipstick on for the needed time. Off set, I never apply it.

But then again, this is Ronit. So I apply the lightest shade of pink I have and look at my reflection in the mirror. And then, I rub almost all of it away. Ronit will have to compromise a little too. Satisfied that I look fairly presentable, I walk out of the loo and make my way to the bar.

There he is. Looking hot as always. My gaze pauses at his lips. The same lips that kissed mine a few days back. I remember every second of it. He is engrossed in his cell phone, a slight frown on his face, and that somehow makes him look even more adorable. But what really has my attention is the fact that he looks so at home here. It is like he belongs here. And it scares me.

Do I have to turn into a female version of him to be with him? Maybe start treating bars as my regular hangout place, take up drinking and smoking full time and maybe even turn into a drug junkie. It would be pretty cool if I start dressing up in all things leather and probably even get some of my body parts pierced, right? And hideous tattoos too.

Shut up. Don't be an idiot. He's just a regular guy and I don't have to degrade myself to be with him. In fact, he does not even seem like someone who smokes or does drugs. And the leather and piercing part was just plain ludicrous to even think of, I chide myself.

Just as I make my way towards him, he looks up from his phone and spots me. I meet his eye and he gives me a tiny wave of his fingers. I smile at him. Just then, a small group of girls approaches him from behind and he turns towards them. From what I can see, it seems like they are asking for his autograph.

And I freeze.

That is what he is. A celebrity. Yes, if we meet tonight and if things go right, we might start dating . . . but . . . this is absurd, isn't it? I'm leaving the guy I love, for a celebrity I'm mad about.

Suddenly, all thoughts about Ronit cease to exist. Ankit. That is what rules my mind. And as if he somehow reads my mind from somewhere, my phone starts to buzz. Maybe it is not so filmy, now that I think of it. He has been calling me almost every hour all day. But the calls had not had an effect of the magnitude that they have on me now. To my intense embarrassment, tears suddenly flooded my eyes. What was I about to do? How did I ever even think that I could exist without Ankit in my life?

I'm simply not capable of doing so. I love him too much.

I turn on my heels and walk out of the club. As the fresh air hits my face, I feel a little alive. I still have Ankit. I still have a life. I will tell him all about everything that has happened. How I had met Ronit and had fallen for him again. How I went on a date with him. How he had kissed me and I had liked it. How I had almost gone on the second date too.

And I would also tell Ankit how I had made up my mind to leave him. How close I had come to doing that. How close I had come to ruining my life. And how terrified I had been when I realized so. I would tell him everything. And I will hope he forgives me. And then, I will forget all about Ronit and pretend we never met.

As I start walking on the sidewalk, my phone buzzes again. Ronit. I don't receive the call. I shouldn't have stood him up, I know. And

I feel bad about doing so. It isn't his fault. I should've been honest with him. I should've told him that I was seeing someone. Someone I loved with all my heart. I shouldn't have led him on. But I cannot bring myself to receive his call and tell him the truth. And I cannot say nothing and just run away either. I send him a text. It says only one word—Sorry.

And then I call Ankit.

'Vatsala?' he asked as soon as he answered.

'Ankit,' was all I could say, as I choked back tears.

'Where have you been? I have been calling all day. Why weren't you taking my calls? Are you okay? I was so worried about you.'

'I'm okay . . . now.'

'Is something wrong? I called Chhavi, but she isn't telling me anything. What happened?' he asks.

'I . . .' I can't say anything. I almost feel too happy to speak. I have Ankit. And he is worried about me. He cares for me. And he loves me. It makes me very, very happy. And I feel a strong liking towards Chhavi. I knew she would never betray me. Maybe I should turn lesbian, after all. It wouldn't be that bad an idea . . .

'Vatsala?' Ankit asked, bringing me back to the present. 'Where are you?'

Prices That We Pay

'Let's go out,' Vatsala said, as she pulled me by my hand.

I applied force to stay on the couch, which had become my permanent residence ever since I broke up with Tushar, almost two months ago. 'I don't want to,' I said.

'You always say no to everything I propose. You never even leave home unless it's for work,' she complains.

'Because I don't want to.'

'Why? You want to spend your entire life on this couch?'

'I wouldn't mind,' I shrugged.

'You're serious,' she said, looking at me with disbelief. 'Have you totally lost it? You're acting like your life's over.'

'It has nothing worth living for anymore.'

'Chhavi. Shut. The. Hell. Up. Why are you getting all melodramatic? People break up every day. They get over it and move on. You have to do the same. Stop acting like this is the first time you broke up with a guy.'

'Yes, this is not my first. But this is the first time it is hurting so much,' I replied honestly.

'Of *course* it hurts. It is *supposed* to hurt. But really, there should be a time-limit. How long do you usually take to get over a break up?'

'Last time it took a week, before that it took just three days, before that—'

'So why is it taking so long this time, then?' she asked.

'Because I *really* love him.'

That shut her up. I loved those moments. The moments when something I said shut Vatsala up. It didn't happen a lot, and I loved it when it did. I wished these moments would last longer, but she recovered really quickly.

'I know the perfect remedy for this!' she shouted.

'And what's that?' I asked, just a little curious. She's so full of all kinds of shit all the time, it's fun seeing the world from her point of view.

'You need to find a stronger love,' she smiled widely.

'I don't think there *exists* a stronger love,' I said but she chose to ignore me.

'Ooh, I'm a genius! Why didn't I think of this before?'

'Think of what?' Now I was seriously excited, not just curious.

'Wait. I'll be back,' she said and left the room. She came back with a handful of DVDs and started reading out the songs from the back and putting them into the music system.

'You think I didn't try this? I did. Eminem's not working,' I said sadly.

'Of course Eminem's not working. He'll work when you need to get some serious attitude and to get all egoistic. Why did you even try him? Listen to *this*. This will work.'

And so, I started listening to *Metallica*. That was all we did all day. And although I did fall in love with it almost instantly, I figured it would take some time to surpass the love I had for Tushar.

I wasn't sure I even *wanted* to get over him. It felt nice loving him. And it felt nice remembering the good times we had had together. If only we hadn't decided to ruin it all by taking everything so seriously. If only we had stuck to keeping our relationship strictly fun.

But that wouldn't have been possible, would it? You simply cannot maintain a purely physical relationship with someone if you really like him. And this was not our regular *like*. It was *love*. The strongest version of it. And so, we just *had to* get into a relationship. And we just *had to* get even more madly in love with each other.

And then, even though we loved each other like crazy, we just *had to* break up. My idea. My stupid, stupid idea. I don't know where I got this whole weird logic from. Tell me, what sense does it make? My moronic theory—*If I can't have enough of him, I don't want any of him.*

How stupid could someone get? Just because I could not deal with missing him *so much of the time*, I took up missing him *all the time*. And made him do the same. He had asked me to not do this. And he had honestly believed that we could have made it work. *But no!* I just *had to* turn a deaf ear. After all, I was 'tired of missing him' so much.

Huh.

I cursed myself all the time for letting him go. No, it wasn't *letting* him go. It was *forcing* him to go. And now, to top everything, he hated me. Had I honestly believed that separation would be better than having a long-distance relationship? Apparently.

But I turned out to be mistaken. *So* mistaken! When we were dating . . . Yes, we had missed each other all the time and we barely ever met and didn't even talk that much. But we *had* each other. We knew that no matter what happened, we had *love*. We had someone to think of before we went to sleep every night. I am not saying he still wasn't the one I thought of every night before I went to sleep. I did. But I was pretty sure he wasn't doing the same. I didn't even know if he was dating someone . . .

Okay, so I won't lie. I had been following him. Not the psycho-stalker following, but you know, just our regular keeping tabs on someone's movements. *Every movement.* I knew he was not dating anyone. Not visibly, at least. There was no rumour of an affair anywhere. He had not been spotted with a date ever since me. That news made me happy.

Another news that made me feel immensely happy and insanely proud was that he had been doing well work-wise. You could find him everywhere those days. Every time I Googled him, I found another new article, singing his praises. He seemed to have taken the Malaysia project seriously. And I was happy for him.

My career was coming along pretty nicely too. Naitik had found me a bunch of interesting, high paying assignments and I had been working on them diligently. Every other day, I received a call from him saying something along the lines of, *'We landed Sunsilk, babes!'* If you are thinking he called everyone 'babes', you are badly mistaken. It was a term he especially reserved for me. (Most others were usually 'assholes' to him.) Even the way he said it was unique. I don't remember him referring to me by my name very often. He did not like 'Chhavi' much, I guess.

Anyway, on the work front, everything was taken care of. Naitik was kicking some serious ass. I found my distraction. Fair game.

But work was the only front of my life that I was doing well at. Otherwise, my life sucked majorly. Sometimes, I felt this strange constriction in my chest . . . and I felt like talking to him. If only I could just hear his voice . . . I had picked up the phone to call him about three million times. But every time I dialled the number, I had chickened out before touching the green 'call' option.

Disturbing questions flooded my mind, not letting me make the call.

What if he says he doesn't love me anymore?

What if he refuses to recognize my voice?

I was happier pretending that he might still secretly love me. And I didn't cherish the thought of calling him and finding otherwise.

Another one of my stupid logics.

At New Year's Eve

31st December 2011

The doorbell chimed and Vatsala rushed to get the door.

'Hey,' she greeted Ankit with a kiss and a hug.

'Hi there,' he said. He entered the apartment, looked at me and smiled. I smiled back. I was used to this; the fake smiles. They came to me naturally now.

'I want to play something for you,' Vatsala said and pulled him by the hand, taking him to her room and making him sit.

I met her eye and winked. She winked back. I showed her my middle finger and went back to my room. I knew what would follow. These guys, Vatsala and Ankit had been together for a year now. It was their first anniversary. And they had been best friends for about five years before getting together. Perfect match, they were. Made for each other.

Whereas, the one made for me was . . . well, *where was he*? Still in Malaysia? Oh no! Wasn't he supposed to come back . . . *today?* He was in town! I automatically picked up my phone to call. Only to keep it down again. Exactly what I had been doing since the last two months.

I had been craving to talk to him. I would have given anything to just get to listen to his voice. But I did not call him even once. I should get an award or something to have this kind of self-control.

I heard Vatsala play something on her guitar in the other room. It was my idea that she learned it. A girl like her, with the kind of destructive mind she had, should never be unoccupied. Devil's workshop, literally.

Seeing them together had somehow started being hard on me. Don't get me wrong, I hadn't turned into a sadist. It was just that, ever since Tushar left . . . seeing these guys together made me realize exactly how pathetic my own life was.

Vatsala hit the last chords on her guitar and silence followed. They must be whispering. And then they would make love. And I would sit there alone, locked up in my room, dreaming about Tushar and wondering what it would have been like, had he been there with me on the New Year's Eve.

No freaking way.

Enough brooding for a lifetime. I was not some sad lonely girl who would sit alone and hope things would work themselves out. It didn't happen that way. You have to *work* to make things right. Exactly what I had *not* been doing since the last couple of months.

If sex was all I could get with Tushar, I would take it. *Something* is better than *nothing,* right? I was willing to agree to any and every kinds and numbers of conditions attached. I didn't care if we could not have a real relationship. I didn't care if we lived miles apart. I didn't care if he didn't love me anymore . . . I loved him and I was prepared to deal with every pain that would come my way if I started it again.

Because I wasn't prepared to live without him anymore.

I picked up my phone again and this time, made the call.

'Hello?' he answered after the fourth ring.

'Tushar . . .'

'Chhavi?'

'Yes,' I said.

'Ohh . . . umm . . . hi.'

'Hi. Are you in town?'

'For the moment, yes.'

I paused for a moment and asked, 'Can we meet?'

'Why?'

I could see that he was angry, and I knew that it would be so. What did I expect, breaking up with him and calling him after two months to ask him to meet? That he would jump at the opportunity and we will somehow just automatically go back to what we were, as if the last two months were just a figment of my imagination?

I remember how mad he had been when I had broken up with him. He seemed more or less in the same frame then too.

'Where are you?' I asked.

He took a moment to reply to that. 'Hawaiian Shack,' he said at last.

'I'll be there in fifteen,' I said and rushed out of the apartment. I didn't care how I looked, I didn't care what I wore. It was coming off quite soon, anyway. Or so I hoped.

And it was just perfect that we were meeting at Hawaiian Shack. That was where we met for the second time that day, after that incident with Valli. And that was where we had got hammered and stoned, and we still were not sure what followed after we had made it to his hotel room.

I would make sure we remembered what happened tonight after we made it to his hotel room. And I would make sure it was awesome enough to make him come back to me for more. We could go back to having a strictly-sexual relationship again, couldn't we? Whatever I could get. Yes, I was desperate. I was dying without him.

As I spotted him in the club, I felt a sudden rush of emotions flood my mind. I saw him sitting there, handsome as ever, and I felt the familiar tinge of pain tug my heart. I had made him go. I had forced him away and now I was paying badly for it.

'Hey,' I said as I approached him.

'Hi,' he said and we had a small awkward moment between us. We didn't know whether to hug, or kiss each other's cheek or shake hands. We ended up shaking hands. *It was plain pathetic.*

'You look good,' I said, meaning it, obviously. He always looked good.

'You too,' he replied, scanning me. I was in faded jeans and a simple peach top. I couldn't be looking good enough to deserve a compliment. But when he said it, I decided to take it at face value. It felt nice.

'Thanks,' the blush was back. Not because of the 'you too' but because of the way his eyes travelled the length of my body. His gaze could still make me shiver. I liked that.

'So . . . how about a drink?' he asked.

'Yeah, sure.'

We ordered our drinks and he looked at me. I could read the question in his eyes. He wanted to know what the sudden meeting was all about. It suited me. I was not in a mood to waste time either.

But before I could say anything, he asked, 'So, how have you been?'

'I am okay. You? The Malaysia project was okay?' I asked, as if I didn't know every bloody detail about every front of his life already.

'Yes! It came along pretty nicely. The producers love it.'

'That's great to know. I remember reading about it somewhere too. Congratulations,' I smiled politely. I couldn't believe this was happening. We were acting *civil*. We were actually being *social* to each other. It hurt me to see that we had reduced to *this*.

'Thank you,' he replied politely.

Before I could say anything else, an anorexic girl who was about as tall as Tushar, came to us and hugged him. I instantly cursed myself for not having greeted him with a hug. It would have given me a valid reason to spend a few seconds in his arms, if nothing else, at least.

When they broke out of the embrace (which was slightly longer than necessary, I noticed) they turned to look at me and Tushar made the introductions. 'Jane, this is Chhavi. Chhavi, Jane.'

'Chhavi! It's so nice to see you,' Jane kissed the air around my cheek and said. 'I have heard *all* about you,' she said.

'You have?' I asked, putting in as much attitude as I could muster. I didn't like the way she had emphasised on *all*.

'Yeah. How could I not?'

I smiled sweetly at her. When all I really wanted to say was—*I have no idea what you are going on about.*

'Let's dance,' she said and pulled Tushar away from me.

Before I could do or say anything, she dragged him to the dance floor. And the next second, I saw them dancing together, amongst several other couples on the floor. They danced right in the middle of the floor and the rest of the couples actually moved away to give them space. Just like you would do for a celebrity.

I could not blame them. Jane did look like a celebrity, which she was. She was at least 5'9" and had a figure of a supermodel, which she so obviously was. And Tushar had always been breathtakingly dashing. So with both of them dancing together on the floor, wasn't it obvious that people would move away to give them space? To make matters even worse, she danced like a rock star. Darn.

By the time the song ended, I was literally green with envy. I could not wait for them to come back, so that I could have Tushar back with me. And when they decided to dance to the next number too, I lost it. I could not take it anymore. I made my way to them and said loudly to Tushar, 'Can I talk to you for a minute?'

'Do you mind waiting till *after* this song?' Jane asked.

'Now?' I asked Tushar, ignoring Jane completely. He looked at me for a while, probably trying to read my expression and decipher what this was all about.

'It's just three minutes!' Jane said.

I kept looking at Tushar. And he kept looking back at me. At last—maybe because he read the *please* etched in bold across my face—he nodded.

'C'mon! You've got to be kidding me! We were having so much fun!' I heard Jane call as we left the dance floor together.

Tushar cleared his throat. 'So . . . umm . . . how's Vatsala?'

'Vatsala is awesome. And so is Ankit. And so is my next door neighbour. And the guy who delivers my milk every day,' I replied.

'I just—'

'Hush. Don't talk. Come with me.'

~

As soon as we got to my apartment, I turned to him.

'Chhavi . . .' Tushar looked uncertain.

'Yeah?' I asked, as I stood in front of him and rested my fingers at the collar of his shirt.

'What are you doing?' he looked surprised. As if it was the first time we were alone in a room.

'What I have been *dying* to do for so long,' I said and ran my hands over the buttons of his shirt.

'Are you serious?' he held my wrist.

'Don't I look it?' I let my fingers tease his chest where they could touch him.

'But *why*?' he held my fingers to make them stop.

'Because it's foolish not to. We both want each other and we know that. So *why not*?' I pulled my hands free of his grasp.

'What if it's too late?' he took a step back.

'I don't think it is.' I took a step forward.

'What if I am seeing someone?' He stopped.

'I don't think you are.' I reached him.

'What makes you think so?' he tilted his head to the side and asked.

'The fact that you are here with me tonight. And no other girl is in sight.' I tilted my head the other way and moved towards him.

And then I kissed him.

I was glad he wasn't stepping backwards or pushing me away anymore. I held the back of his neck and pulled him closer. And even though he didn't push me away, he didn't invite me either. But I didn't lose hope. I knew I had to work my way back into his heart. I had hurt him before, and he was trying to save himself from getting hurt again. But I wasn't threatened by the fact. In fact, it gave me enough drive to try harder, till I won him over again. And soon, it showed results.

So I just kept kissing him, giving my everything into that kiss. It was not like I was not enjoying it, but that was not what I was aiming for. My intention was to make *him* enjoy it more. To make him enjoy it enough to want more.

It felt amazing when he held my chin and actually *participated* in the kiss. We had kissed after so long, that I had almost forgotten how good we were together, the same way I always seemed to forget how handsome he was. I was surprised to find him *that good*. Or maybe it was just my deprivation that was having that effect.

His hand held the hair at the back of my head and pulled me forward, towards him. My body moulded itself in his and we fit together like a pair. I felt sexy. His other hand slowly moved downwards, grazing my neck. His fingertips touching my skin. Lightly. Making me want more. His fingers lingered at the base of my neck and I had to take a calming breath in order to prevent myself from passing out.

The sheer anticipation of what would follow was enough to make my weak in the knees. I tightened my hold on him, to support myself. My knees were about to buckle. His hand moved lower and pulled the strings of my top. We let it fall. He looked into my eyes and I stared right back. And then, his eyes moved lower.

What followed was definitely our best lovemaking.

My body responded to his touch as if it recognized it. It almost felt like my body had been *missing* his touch. The way his fingers ran all over my body left me shivering. The way his tongue explored my neck had me wanting for more. I suddenly realized how totally and completely I was in love with him. It scared me. But I forced all such thoughts out of my mind. I had to live in the present and stop fretting about the future. It was high time.

My body welcomed his touch.

I felt at home.

~

I opened my eyes slowly. As I remembered what had happened the previous night, a slow smile crept on my face. It was bliss. Having Tushar back. Well, yes, of course I knew I did not have him back yet. But I was sure I would. Now that I had him in bed, next to me, I was sure I could convince him that I regretted what I had done. That I had been an idiot and I knew . . .

Wait a minute, where was Tushar? As I turned on my side, I could not see him in bed. *Washroom* was the first thought that came to my mind. But when I checked, I found out that he wasn't there. I looked around and couldn't see any article of his clothing, shoes or cell phone lying around. I rushed to the window.

There he was.

But who was that girl he was hugging? *Jane.* As I looked down from the window, I saw him make his way out of the building and straight into Jane's arms. He then stood there, talking to her for a couple of minutes before they got into a car together and left.

I stood there for a few minutes, transfixed, staring at nothing. My brain froze for some time. And then, I struggled to put pieces together and understand the situation. *What just happened?* Was Tushar dating Jane? Everything that had happened implied so. She had been edgy while talking to me, Tushar had not wanted me to meet him at the club, and once there, he was unwilling to talk to me . . . he did not want to come back to my apartment . . . or make love. Then he had left first thing in the morning, without waking me up . . . *with her.*

I could not believe what I had done. They were dating and I had forced him to cheat on her. I had not even asked him if they were together. I had just assumed that he did not have a girlfriend. And without thinking, I had gone ahead and slept with him. Had I honestly believed that making out first and talking later was a better option?

I felt like a slut.

That was when I decided to stop. For real. For forever. I picked up my phone and tried to blink away the tears flooding my eyes. After several failed attempts, I finally was able to type the message. It was the last thing I would ever say to Tushar.

What we had together was nice.
I hope you have a wonderful life.

I hit *send.*
A part of me died.

To Square One

'Don't be such a snob. Go get ready,' Vatsala said.

'I don't want to go out! You guys go,' I protested.

'We're not asking you whether or not you want to come with us. We're telling you that you're coming with us,' Allya joined allies with Vatsala.

'But—'

'No buts! You just *have* to come,' Vatsala insisted.

'Can't we do this later?' I asked, looking up at her hopefully. I was lying on my couch as usual and they were standing in front of it, looking down at me. Their expressions told me that I looked like shit. They even had the slight frown that people have when they look at the filth at the sides of railway stations.

'Shut up, Chhavi. Enough of all this. It is already the middle of January and you are still asking us to postpone this?' Vatsala looked at me as if I was the craziest person on the planet.

'Exactly. This is supposed to be our New Year's celebration. We're already two weeks late,' Allya said.

'I just don't feel like going out tonight—'

'You don't feel like going out *ever*,' Allya shouted, looking exasperated. What? I had just lost the love of my life. A part of me had died and my life wasn't worth living anymore. And they expected me to go *celebrate* with them? And whenever I said no, they looked at me as if I was some kind of a hopeless lunatic.

'Come. You don't have a choice,' Vatsala met my eye and said softly.

I looked at their determined faces. No, I did *not* have a way out of this. And going out with them would keep them from pestering me again for at least another couple of weeks. Fair deal.

I thought I would just go wear something off the rack and somehow go through the night. Maybe drinking would help. I wondered why I did not think of it before. Wasn't that what people did after they had a break up? Drink? Wasn't that the one tested remedy to heal broken hearts? That is one thing I would try.

I had tried Metallica. And it helped, really. As long as you are listening to *Ride the Lightening*, everything in your life is perfect. Nothing can touch you. But once you stop, everything comes back. So I found a solution—now, I play Metallica all day all night long. And yes, there is no greater love.

But still, thoughts of this one guy always come back . . .

'Wear this,' Vatsala said, removing a dress from her cupboard and pushing it towards me.

I was stunned. I stared at the dress, disbelievingly. My eyes were playing tricks on me. This couldn't be. This *just* couldn't be. Finally, when I regained my power of speech, I whispered, 'Is this the Fendi dress? Is this *my* Fendi dress?'

'Yes!' Allya said.

'How?' I asked. I was feeling weak in the knees. Shallow, yes, but sometimes awesome articles of clothing have that effect on me.

'We knew you wanted it. So we—' Allya started, but Vatsala cut her off mid-sentence with, 'So we . . . pooled our resources and bought this for you.'

'Really? That's so sweet of you,' I looked at them and smiled.

'And you still weren't ready to go out with us . . .'

'Stop your drama, Vatsala! I am coming. You should have shown me the dress *before* to hasten up the process!' I laughed.

I loved these girls. Those past two weeks, I had been a mess. Real mess. I did not eat, drink, sleep, or do anything at all. If not for them, I would have carried on like that forever. But they had been adamant on pulling me out of my depression. They had been there, by my side when I blasted *The Unforgiven II* on the music system at full volume in the middle of the night. They had been there to handle things when the neighbours had come to complain.

They had been there when I cried at nights, tears flowing relentlessly down my cheeks. They had passed me tissues. They had cried with me. They had made me eat. They had forced me into the shower. They had made me laugh. They had exhausted me with all kinds off bullshit that seemed to flow from them, and made me sleep out of boredom, if nothing else.

And finally, they were getting successful in forcing me to get off the couch. Whoever says that friendship between girls is shallow and superficial has no freaking idea what he is talking about. We can be true friends to each other too. And Vatsala and Allya had proved it.

I loved them.

~

'What are we doing at Marine Beach?' I asked and looked at them questioningly. We were walking along the sea, side by side and it had started to get all weird. I mean—I was wearing a bronze coloured Fendi dress. And it glittered. And I had to remove my stilettoes as their heels dug into the sand. I didn't think I loved the girls anymore.

'Getting some fresh air. Soaking in the scenery,' Allya said.

'The natural beauty. The sunset,' Vatsala joined in.

'The—'

'Shut up, both of you! Tell me—why am I wearing this dress?' I asked. They had made me wear that dress to take me to Marine Drive? Had they totally lost it?

'Umm . . . sudden change of plans,' Vatsala said and Allya nodded her head vigorously in agreement. 'We were planning for a dance club before . . . but then—'

'Vatsala. Dance club? *You*?' I raised my eyebrow. Something was definitely up.

'Yeah. I mean—it was for *you*, not for *me*. So I decided to deal with it,' she shrugged. She was really a very bad liar. A four-year-old could have seen through the façade.

I stopped walking and turned to give them a deadly stare.

'Two minutes, and you will know,' Allya said and motioned something to Vatsala.

'We'll see you,' Vatsala said and they both started to leave.

'You're *going*?' I asked. It wasn't just curiosity anymore. It was getting creepy.

'Two minutes,' Allya said again.

'But—?'

'Just wait,' they said and started leaving. 'And by the way. We were not the ones who got you that dress.'

I had no idea what was going on. They had dragged me out of the apartment, forced me into this gorgeous dress, to a *beach*. And only to leave me there and run away? And what did they mean they were not the ones who got me that dress? *What the hell was going on?* I did not have to wait for long to find out.

Just as I made to follow them, I saw Tushar coming towards us, looking handsome as ever, of course.

'Thank God,' Vatsala let out. 'We were beginning to think you would never come.'

'How could I not?' Tushar said, with his eyes fixed on me.

I felt my body shiver. Because of the way he looked at me, of course. The only difference was that the shiver wasn't in a *good* way. The way he looked at me scared me. You know the look a predator has when it looks at its prey? Exactly. He looked ready to pounce at me any minute. And not for sex, mind you. *To kill.*

'So . . . we should go?' Vatsala asked, looking at us.

He nodded. *'Please don't,'* I shouted in my mind. I could not say it aloud. I was not capable. My power of speech was left hindered. Man, was I scared! As soon as the girls left, I turned and started to walk away. That was the only way I could think of to protect myself. I was so sure he was going to kill me.

He joined me. We walked for a while, next to each other, saying nothing. I was reminded of the last time we were there. Right there, at that point twenty feet to my right, he had told me *he thinks he loves me.* And we had started dating. And life had been awesome. Then I had screwed it all up. *Moron.*

'Why are you here, Tushar?'

'To talk about us,' he said.

'There *is* no *us.*'

'You think?' he cocked his head back and asked, as if challenging me to answer in the negative.

'Stop fooling around. Go back.'

'You ask me to go away a lot, have you noticed?'

We did not say anything for a while. I could not understand why he had met me. If he had taken the pains of letting Vatsala and Allya in on the plan to meet me here, something must be up. But it did not seem like he wanted to answer that right away. He was having fun messing with me. Well, okay. It gave me more time with him. Suited me.

'I thought you forgot about me,' I said. He had not called me even once since *that* morning. There was no mention of the text I had sent him. Nothing to say that we had slept together that night.

'Me? I thought *you* rejected me.'

'*Reject* you? *I* rejected you?' I asked.

'Yeah. Your SMS. It was a *goodbye* in every word of it.'

'Well, you can't blame me. You went with Jane! Your *girlfriend*,' I accused.

'Jane is not my girlfriend!'

'You broke up?' I asked. So was that what it was all about? Now that they had separated, he had come back to me? Had they broken up because of me? I felt like shit.

'*Break up?* What are you talking about? We were never even together.'

'C'mon, Tushar. Don't lie to me. That night, I was there at the club with you. I saw the way you guys danced together. And next morning, I saw you leave with her.'

'Yes, we danced. Because we are friends. She was a model at the Malaysia project, so we had spent two months together on that assignment. That night, everyone associated with the project was there. So was she. And we danced. Big deal!' Tushar let out.

'But, next morning . . . .?'

'We had some things to wrap up. We were supposed to meet at the company's office and since I overslept, she came to pick me up. As simple as that!'

'Oh,' I said. *They weren't dating. They weren't dating. They weren't dating.* I cheered mutely at the thought.

'You thought I was going out with her? Shit. So, that's why the *goodbye* message?'

I nodded again.

'Idiot.'

We walked on the beach, side by side, pondering over the respective revelations we had made. I felt good. A lot better than I had been feeling recently. We decided telepathically to start the conversation all over again. We somehow started with small talk.

'You look good,' he said. And this time when his eyes travelled my body, the shiver I felt was a pleasant one. I mean, come on. I was wearing the gorgeous Fendi dress—the dress *he* gifted me. And he was there to see me in it. Wasn't I entitled to feel that pleasant shiver?

'Thanks,' I whispered. 'You? Been okay? Work going well?'

'Yeah. Actually . . . I am thinking of taking up the Chrome offer.'

'Really?'

'Yes. It is a good deal. A solid two year contract. I need something permanent.'

I nodded.

'I am looking for a place around here . . .' he said.

'Great!' I smiled brightly. Too brightly. He was taking up the Chrome project. And it is a two year contract. And I knew this for a fact that it was in Mumbai. *What is this all about?* I wondered. He had come to meet me. In fact, he had *arranged* to meet me, with Vatsala and Allya in on the plan, and then he had mentioned that he was taking up a job that required him to spend most of the next two years in Mumbai.

Is this about what I think it's about? Naah. Don't be foolish. I didn't dare to hope.

'We need to talk,' he said seriously. 'After all the time we spent together, after all the amazing moments we had, the times we laughed, the things we did, the way we loved . . . you describe our relationship as "nice"?'

'What?' I was taken aback. What was he going on about?

'The text you sent me that morning?' he said.

'Oh.' That rang a bell. *What we had together was nice.*

'I mean. First—you came to me and literally dragged me to bed. And then—next morning, you leave me this stupid text? Care to explain what that was all about?' he cocked his head back to look at me.

'The text wasn't stupid,' was all I could think of saying. 'I meant what I said.'

'So you do want me to have a wonderful life ahead?'

'Of course.' *I hope you have a wonderful life.*

'Impossible. Unless you are in it, with me . . . my life can't be wonderful.'

I stopped to look at him. He looked serious. I asked, 'You want to take me back?'

'I never let you go.'

I stared at him.

'I could not leave you, because I loved you too much. And I knew you loved me. But you were scared. So I decided to take the lead and get our lives back on track. You think I worked like a maniac on the Malaysia project because I cared about my career? No! I worked on it because I knew if I did well, I would get the Chrome project. And I needed it. For *us*.'

I still stayed silent, continuing to stare at him.

'I never believed in love and relationships. *Until you.* You made me realize what I had been missing out on. You taught me what love is. And you made me want to experience it. And I did. With you. I can't fall out of it now. Baby, I see my future in you. I see my life in you. Without you, my life has nothing. I need you back. Now.'

'Tushar . . .' I could hardly whisper his name.

'I'm thinking of getting a place here, Chhavi. We can be closer. We can have a real relationship.'

'Have you made up your mind?' I asked.

'It depends . . . on whether or not you want me to.'

I could not believe it was happening. Just an hour ago, I had been lying face down on my couch, thinking that my life was over and there was not anything worth living for anymore. Except Metallica and pizzas. And suddenly, out of the blue, I got back the person I loved the most in the world. I got my life back. And I got the Fendi dress too. Which was almost equally amazing. *Almost.*

'Would you like that?' he prodded, and I realized that he was waiting for a reply.

'I can't believe this is happening,' I spoke my mind.

'Well, it is,' he smiled at me.

'I like it!' My grin was wider than ever.

'I think I like it too!'

'I love you,' I said and hugged him tight. *This is it. I am never letting him go. I have made that mistake before. Twice. And I have paid. Now, I am stopping. I will not think too much about the future and would live in the present instead,* I decided. I had Tushar back. I was thrilled.

'We can make out whenever we want now,' he said.

'Oh? So this is about the sex?'

'Uh-huh. And the dirty talk.'

'Jerk,' I said and shook my head.

'The getting drunk and stoned.'

'Hey—'

'I'll miss the phone sex though,' he said regretfully.

'Tushar—'

'And the video chatting.'

'Stop,' I smiled and punched him playfully on the arm.

'We never did get dirty on Skype, after all,' he continued, not budging.

Oh God. I *so* loved him.

Epilogue

Six months later

'You look cute,' I said, looking at Allya's reflection in the mirror. Cute was an understatement. She looked *out of the world*. And she should have too, of course. It was her wedding, after all.

Yes! Allya was getting married! It was an arranged marriage. Her parents, like mine, had been pressurizing her on getting married since ages. Only, I did not pay any heed to mine, while she agreed to meet the guy. Harshvardhan, the guy, was nothing like the disaster that was my arranged marriage proposal. He was the exact opposite. As in—*out of the world*, in a *good* way. Tall and handsome. Fair, though. (Vatsala had a tiny crush on him, I guess.)

And Harshvardhan had also turned out to be *royalty*. A *real* prince. His parents descended from some kind of posh, royal family or something. Of course, Allya had liked him. And of course, he liked her back. Didn't I tell you how smashing she looked? So, it was hardly a surprise that Harshvardhan's family had liked her instantly. And the wedding was set, in no time.

I think his family had not seen the condoms ad she had once done. And I hoped that they would never.

'I do?' Allya asked nervously.

'Of course! I mean, look at you! You are all set to blow everyone away tonight,' I smiled.

'No,' she shook her head and looked at me. 'You look better than me.'

'Aww. No, you look amazing,' I said. We were dressed in heavy lehangas and had loaded ourselves with insanely expensive jewellery and applied make-up like we had seen the princesses do in those *Jodhaa Akbar* like historical movies. After all, we were in Jaipur, attending a royal wedding in a huge palace. Justified.

'I am serious. You are looking better than me. Do something with the make-up. Or get rid of some jewellery. You can*not* look better than me. It is *my* wedding,' she panicked.

I instantly started removing some of the bangles from my arms. Though I secretly wanted to look awesome. Tushar was downstairs, at the wedding hall. Still, I should have dressed down a little. It wasn't fair to Allya. It was her day.

'Is this okay?' I asked after I removed a few more articles of my jewellery and lightened my make-up. Bright red lipstick was a bad idea anyway.

'I guess,' she said uncertainly.

'Now?' I asked readjusting my lehanga in a way that made me look less like a bride. *Shit.*

'Yeah, better,' she nodded and turned to Vatsala. 'What do you think?'

'Of what?' Vatsala asked and looked up at us. She had no clue what we were talking about. I felt pity for her. Poor soul. She was caught up in her own clothes. And jewellery. And make-up.

'I asked Chhavi to go a little lighter on the jewellery and make-up. Tell me, do I look better than her?' Allya asked Vatsala.

But Vatsala didn't even look at her. She stood there, staring at me instead, with an unreadable expression on her face.

'Vatsala? Are you listening? Are you okay?' I asked.

After two whole minutes of silence, she finally whispered, 'Can I go a little *light* on the jewellery and the make-up too?'

We burst out laughing.

'Of course,' I said and shook my head.

'You scared me there, for a minute,' Allya said and turned back to the mirror.

'Thank God.' The look on Vatsala's face said just one thing—relief.

'Now tell me! Do I look better than Chhavi?' Allya prodded again. She was getting really nervous. For no reason. She was looking prettier than any girl I had seen in my life. And I was a model, and saw a lot of pretty faces on a regular basis.

'Of course, you do! Why are you even worrying?' Vatsala replied, now back to her usual self. I went to help her get rid of the neckpieces she was stuck in.

'Really?' Allya asked.

'Really,' we replied together.

Vatsala winked at me. Allya had been fretting about looking the best amongst the three of us ever since we had first started looking for our outfits for the wedding. And even though we knew perfectly well that we would never look as good as her anyway, we had felt nice just thinking that Allya felt we *could*. But then, her panic had started to rise. And I had made a pact with Vatsala—we would always say that Allya looked way better than either of us. We would not be lying, anyway.

I winked back, just as my phone beeped. I received a text message from Naitik—

Where the fuck is my favourite client? Get your ass back to the office, you need to be spanked. I fetched Levi Strauss for you, babes! I need your autograph on the agreement papers!

Wow. I got Levi's! This guy is really a miracle-worker. Just as I turned to tell the girls the good news, my phone beeped again. I had received another text message from that miracle-worker agent of mine.

And just btw, I know you are off somewhere with that guy of yours. And I still haven't received a single video from you.

I adored him.

As we went down the stairs, walking on either side of Allya, I shared a secret smile with Vatsala. We were happy. Truly, completely happy. Things had turned out better than planned. Everything around us was awesome. Our eyes scanned the room and stopped at the most beautiful sights in the world. For Allya—Harshvardhan. For me—Tushar. And for Vatsala—Ronit. *Yes! They got together.*

Naah, kidding! Ankit was still her knight in shining armour. Had it not been so, she would have been dead. I would have taken care of that personally.

My gaze paused at Tushar, who looked even hotter in the ethnic getup. He looked at me appreciatively and smiled. A shiver ran up my spine, just as it always did.

Life was perfect.